Passing Strange

PASSING STRANGE

ELLEN KLAGES

A TOM DOHERTY ASSOCIATES BOOK
NEW YORK

This is a work of fiction. All of the characters, organizations, and
events portrayed in this novella are either products of the author's
imagination or are used fictitiously.

A Tor.com Book
Published by Tom Doherty Associates
175 Fifth Avenue
New York, NY 10010

www.tor.com

Tor® is a registered trademark of
Macmillan Publishing Group, LLC.

ISBN 978-0-7653-8951-0 (ebook)
ISBN 978-0-7653-8952-7 (trade paperback)

First Edition: January 2017

For Emma and Eunice, Duke Hobson,
and the rest of the cast at
Polyvinyl Films

THE MODERN CITY

One

On the last Monday of her life, Helen Young returned from the doctor's and made herself a cup of tea. As she had expected, the news was not good; there was nothing more that could be done.

From the windows of her apartment high atop Nob Hill, San Francisco's staggered terraces lay like a child's blocks, stacked higgledy-piggledy, the setting sun turning glass and steel into orange neon, old stone and stucco walls glowing with a peach patina. The fog coiled though the hills like a white serpent.

She set the delicate porcelain cup onto a teak side table and thought about what she needed to accomplish. Her final To-Do list. Ivy, her companion-slash-caregiver, had the day off, which made the most important task both simpler and more challenging. She would not have to explain, but would have to do it all herself.

Perhaps she should wait until morning? Helen debated, then picked up her phone. After seventy-five years, she was the last one standing; this was no time for missteps or procrastination. She tapped the screen and summoned a cab.

The day had been warm, as autumn in the City often was, but the fog would chill the evening air. She slipped on a light wool jacket and glanced at the brass-headed cane leaning against the side of the sofa. Would she need it, or would it be an impediment?

Even though her hearing was shot, and her glasses were as thick as a cartoon's, her legs were still good, for an old broad. Hell, her legs were still *great*. She wrapped a hand around the dragon handle and did a nice buck-and-wing, then set the tip down onto the hardwood and left it where it was.

At the apartment's door, she stopped. If anything did go wrong—

She backtracked to the kitchen and the tiny whiteboard that hung next to the fridge, and scribbled an address under ENSURE and TUNA. Easy to erase when she came back. Easy to find if she didn't.

The doorman escorted her to the waiting cab. "Chinatown," she said to the driver. "Spofford Alley, between Washington and Clay." She heard the cabbie sigh. A trip of less than half a mile was not the fare he'd hoped.

"Off the main drag," he said. "What's there?"

"Long-lost friends," Helen answered, and smiled as if that brought her both joy and sorrow.

San Francisco was a city of great density, as much vertical as horizontal, surrounded on four sides by water, houses cheek-to-jowl, but Chinatown made the rest seem spacious. More than seventy thousand people packed into a single square mile. Grant Avenue was a string of gaudy shops and restaurants catering to the tourist trade. The alleys were not as gilded or sanitized. As the cab turned into the single, cramped block lined with three-story brick buildings on either side, Helen could smell the distinctive blend of spices and dried things, vinegar and garbage.

"Stop here," she said.

"Are you sure, lady? This isn't a safe neighborhood, especially after dark."

"I've never been more certain."

"Suit yourself." He glanced at the meter. "That'll be four-ten."

She handed a twenty through the window in the thick Plexiglas that separated driver and passenger. "Wait here—I should be about fifteen minutes. There'll be another of those for my return trip."

"Sign says No Stopping, Tow-Away."

"If the cops come, circle the block." She slid another twenty through.

"Got it." The cabbie nodded his assent, and Helen got out.

In the dusk of early evening, the alley seemed to be made of shadows, the only illumination a few lights in upper-story windows across the pavement, laundry hanging from the sills, and an illuminated mirror in the back of a beauty salon two doors down, a CLOSED sign dangling in its dingy window. Number 38 was a shabby building with brickwork painted the color of dried blood; a narrow door and street-level window were covered with thick plywood painted to match. The entrance was a solid, weathered slab without ornamentation, not even a knocker. It bore no signs of recent use.

"You know someone who actually *lives* here?" the cabbie asked from his open window.

"Not precisely," Helen replied. She removed a ring of keys from her jacket pocket. "I inherited the building, a long time ago."

The vestibule was dark. Helen closed the outer door and took a Maglite from the pocket of her trousers. In a hallway darker still, she used another key to unlock a wooden door whose hinges screeched with disuse. A flight of rickety steps led down; an odor of must and damp earth wafted up.

She flicked the switch at the top of the stairs, bare bulbs glaring on, and turned off her tiny light. Holding the railing for support, she made her careful way down into the cellar.

The floor below was cement. Helen's sensible, rubber-soled shoes made no sound. She went through an archway and turned left, then left again. Her progress was slow, but steady. It was a maze down here, easy to get disoriented. At one time, most of the buildings on the street had been connected underground, six or seven strung together by invisible passages.

The "ghost tours" run for the tourists claimed that these were all dens of iniquity—opium and white slavery. That might have been true before the 1906 fire. But after? Speakeasies, perhaps, until Prohibition was repealed, or just convenient ways to get from one place to another. In those days, the cops needed no excuse for a raid in *China*town, and the subterranean routes were a matter of survival.

Now these were only storerooms. The electric lights ended at the third turn. She took out the Maglite again. Its narrow beam caught the edges of shrouded furniture, cardboard boxes, an iron-bound trunk, and more than a few scuttling rats. The LEDs gave everything an eerie blue cast, and she shivered despite herself.

One more turn led her into a small room with a dirt floor. Two walls were stone, one brick, all solid. The door she'd come through was the only opening. Helen shone the light onto the brick wall. Its regular expanse was broken only by a wooden rack that held a motley array of dusty teacups and bowls, stacks of chipped plates. A rusty-lidded cast-iron pot sagged the boards of the middle shelf.

She switched the light to her left hand and focused the beam on the pot. She reached behind it and found the small knob hidden by its bulk. She tugged; the knob did not move. With a sigh, she tucked the light under one arm, awkwardly trying to keep it focused. She gave silent thanks for the yoga and dance classes that kept her as flexible as she was. Using both hands, she tugged at the unseen latch. It finally slid open with a click so soft she barely heard it, even in the silence of the underground chamber.

Helen stepped back as a section of the brick wall pivoted outward, creating an opening just wide enough for a person to slip through. It had been formed of the bricks themselves, the alternating blocks creating a crenulated edge to the secret doorway. She felt the hair on her neck spike at the touch of cool air, damp and old and undisturbed.

It had been built for illicit deliveries of whiskey, back in the '20s, she'd been told, a clandestine tunnel leading all the way to Stockton Street. By the time *she'd* first seen it, it was just a dead end. Now she was the only person alive who knew it existed. Soon it would be another lost bit of history. She switched the light back to her right hand and stepped into the opening.

Three feet beyond was a wall, a deep niche the size of a small window hewn into the rock-studded cement.

It looked like a crypt, a singular catacomb. But a crypt holds the remains of the dead. This, she thought, was a vault, its contents of—inestimable—value.

Her light revealed a wooden crate, slightly larger than a *LIFE* magazine, two inches thick, covered in dust. Helen brushed it off, then slid her hands under the thin wood and lifted it. It was not heavy, just a bit ungainly. She held the Maglite tight against one edge, and stepped backward into the room with the crockery. The cane would *definitely* have been a nuisance.

She rested the edge of the crate on one of the shelves and stared into the vault for a long moment, seeing something far beyond the stone. Then she shook herself, as if waking, and reached behind the iron pot. Reversing the latch was easier. Another soft *click,* and the doorway slowly slid closed for the last time, the jagged edges of its bricks fitting perfectly into the pattern of their stationary counterparts.

An oversized shopping bag with paper handles lay folded on the shelf with the teacups. She slid the crate into it, laying it flat. Holding the bag like a tray, she walked back through the labyrinth of turns, moving much more slowly. With the last of her energy she trudged up the stairs into the gloomy vestibule, leaving the door ajar. No longer anything of value down there. She stepped back out into Spofford Alley. Even at night, the narrow, dimly lit street seemed bright and expansive after the darkness of the cellars below.

Helen laid the bag on the backseat of the waiting cab, and locked the outside door with a relieved sigh. *That* was done. Handing the cabbie the promised bill, she got in. When they neared her building, she tapped on the Plexiglas. "Use the back entrance, please."

The service elevator took her to the twelfth floor, avoiding the doorman and any questions, and she let herself into the silent apartment. Setting the bag on her dresser, she went to the kitchen, erased the address from the whiteboard, and poured herself three fingers of the eighteen-year-old Macallan. Much more than her usual nightcap. Ivy would tsk and scold, but Ivy wasn't there. Helen took a screwdriver from a drawer and returned to the bedroom.

Her drink was half gone before she felt ready. She laid a towel on her bed and gently withdrew the crate from the bag. The screws were old, set deeply into each side. The thin wood splintered as she removed them, one by one. When the last screw lay on the towel, she used her fingers to carefully remove the lid.

Inside lay a silk-wrapped rectangle, nearly as large as the crate. She lifted it out and set it on the end of her bed, untying the cord that had secured the four corners of the fabric like the top of a circus tent. The silk slipped off onto the comforter, revealing the shallow glass-topped box within.

Helen stared, then downed the last of the scotch in one long swallow.

"Hello, you," she said. "It's been a while."

Two

Tuesdays were always slow. Marty Blake had no idea why. He was behind the front counter, catching up on paperwork—printing out mailing labels, updating the catalog and the database—when he heard the jingle of the bell over the door.

Foot traffic was better since he'd moved to his new location. Not that there hadn't been plenty of people on the streets of the Tenderloin, just not the clientele he wanted. Martin Blake Rare Books was a tiny shop, and the rent was astronomical, but only a few blocks from Union Square, so chances were excellent that any customers could afford whatever they fancied.

He looked up to see an elderly Asian woman step softly inside. One hand gripped the head of an antique cane; the other held a large Neiman Marcus shopping bag. She wore black silk trousers and blouse under a cream jacket with lapels embroidered in a deep red that matched her lipstick.

This one had money, all right. On the far side of eighty—he couldn't tell at a glance just how far—her face was wizened and her hair was thin, but still inky black, shot with a few strands of white. She wasn't stooped or hunched, and although the hand on the cane was spotted with age, her eyes were bright bits of jet behind thick silver-rimmed glasses.

He straightened his own jacket and ran a quick finger through his goatee as she approached. "May I help you?"

"Your specialty is twentieth-century ephemera." It was not a question.

He shrugged. "One of my areas of expertise. Are you looking for something in particular?"

"Perhaps. May I leave this here?" She eased her bag onto a table.

"Be my guest."

She nodded her thanks, and Marty returned to his accounts. No need to keep a shoplifting eye out for this one.

Fifteen minutes passed, punctuated only by the tappings of her cane on the hardwood floor and his fingers on the keyboard. Marty looked up occasionally, watching her peruse the shelves, trying to get an idea of what she was drawn to. Much of his business was online, and the bulk of his inventory was in storage. He only had room to display his most select pieces.

In locked golden-oak cases and shallow, glass-topped tables, illuminated by tasteful halogen spots, were fewer than a hundred items. First editions, signed prints, and a few original manuscripts and drawings filled the front of the house. Some less respectable items—early paperbacks, erotica, some golden-age comics—still rare and valuable, but not to everyone's taste, were in secure cabinets that lined the back wall.

One held a dozen pulp magazines from the '20s and '30s—garish covers, lurid scenes of murder and torture featuring scantily clad women with eyes like snake-filled pits, bound or chained and menaced by hunchbacked fiends, Oriental villains, mad scientists. Every issue was in pristine condition. They'd been packed away in boxes for years, but in the last decade, the market had skyrocketed enough to justify the display space.

The old lady had returned to the back wall twice now. The Christie mapback, maybe? He didn't see her as a pulp fan. Those were usually geeky men buying up their fantasies with Silicon Valley start-up money that had blossomed into stock options.

Finally she turned and pointed. "May I see this one?"

Damn. Really? You never knew in this business. It *was* a pulp, and the best one of the lot, but the last thing he'd have thought she'd like—a 1936 *Weird Menace* whose cover was legendary for its grotesquerie.

He kept the surprise out of his voice. "Certainly." He unlocked the cabinet, removing the tray case and setting it on a nearby table. He adjusted a rheostat and a halogen circle brightened for close inspection.

She sat, leaning her cane against the side of her chair, and gazed at the magazine in front of her with an expression Marty couldn't read. Reverence? Longing? A bit of excitement, but mixed with—what? She looked almost homesick. He sat down across from her.

"Tell me about this," she said.

"Well, as you can see, it's in superb condition. White pages, crisp spine, as if it were fresh off the newsstand." He slid a hand beneath the mylar sleeve and tilted the magazine slightly. "It's an excellent issue, stories by both Clark Ashton Smith *and* Manly Wade Wellman, which alone makes it quite collectible, since—"

She held up a hand. "I have no interest in those stories," she said. "What about that *cover*?"

It was a violent scene with a dark, abstract background. The subject was a pale woman, her eyes wide with fear, naked except for a wisp of nearly flesh-toned silk, a nest of green-scaled vipers coiled around her feet. Looming over her, a leering hooded figure in scarlet brandished a whip. It was a terrifying, erotic illustration, one that left *nothing*—and at the same time, everything—to the viewer's imagination.

"*Ah.*" The art. Marty smoothly changed his sales pitch. "The artist is, of course, Haskel. The signature's at the bottom right, there." He pointed to an angular **H**, the crossbar a rising slash with ASKEL underneath. "He did close to a hundred covers, not just for *Weird Menace,* but for several of the other—" He groped for the word. "—unconventional—magazines. A lot of output for a short career—just seven years. No one really knows why he stopped." He thought back to the reference books in his office. "His last cover was in 1940. October or November, I think."

"Nothing after that?"

"Not a trace. It's like he disappeared off the face of the earth." He recalled conversations he'd had with other dealers over the years. "There are rumors," he said slowly, "that he did do one last cover, but it was never published. No one even knows what house it was for. I've heard guys at Pulpcon sit in the bar and talk about it like it was the Holy Grail, the one piece *any* collector would hock his grandmother for." He stopped, remembering who he was talking to. "No offense, ma'am."

"None taken. What do *you* think happened?"

"The war, probably. Might have been killed, but there's no service record."

She nodded. "My husband was a pilot. His plane was never found."

"I'm sorry. But, for Haskel, there's no paperwork of *any* kind, other than a few invoices. No photos, either.

He's a bit of a mystery."

"I see. And—?" She looked at him expectantly.

Marty thought back to the few articles that had been published about Haskel. "He worked almost exclusively in chalk pastels, not oils, which make his paintings smoother and softer, with an almost—" What *had* that reviewer said? Marty drummed his fingers. Ah, yes. "—an almost Technicolor *glow*. His style is unmistakable, and this is considered one of his finest covers."

He lifted the magazine once more, this time placing it into the old woman's hands. "The detail is exquisite."

"If you like that sort of thing." The woman arched an eyebrow. "How much?"

He thought quickly. The catalog listing was eight hundred, but he'd seen the look on her face. "In this condition, twelve hundred."

"That seems reasonable," she said.

Marty breathed a sigh of relief. Was she even going to *try* and haggle? If not, it would be an excellent Tuesday after all.

"But I'm afraid my interest lies in the original artwork." The old woman returned the magazine to the tray case.

Marty sputtered, then coughed in surprise. "An original *Haskel*? Almost impossible." He shook his head. "I've only seen one, at an exhibition. There are five, maybe six known to exist."

"You claimed there were nearly a hundred covers," the woman said in an imperious, indignant tone.

"That's what he painted, yes. But—" Marty produced a handkerchief and wiped his dampening forehead. "You see, back then, the pulp market was the lowest of the low. As soon as the magazine was on the stands, the art was destroyed. It had no value to anyone, including the artists. Besides, chalk pastels aren't as—sturdy—as oil paint. Delicate as a butterfly wing."

"There *are* originals for sale?"

"Not often. They're all in private collections. The last one that came up at auction was five years ago, and it went for $60,000. One might go for double that, now."

"Really?" She tapped a finger to her lips, thinking, and then smiled with an expression so expansive it pleated her entire face. "I'll just fetch my shopping bag, young man. I believe I have something that will interest you."

Three

As she put the bag onto the table, Helen watched the man with a distaste she was careful to conceal. After twenty-seven years as a judge, she was well practiced in giving no clue to her thoughts. She had an excellent poker face.

Martin Blake was a small man with thinning, gelled hair—not *quite* a comb-over—beady eyes, and a ridiculous little beard. He wore an off-the-rack jacket over a print shirt and a pair of "designer" jeans, none of which were to her taste. From his speech about the magazine, she had sized him up as a man whose belief in his own expertise was inflated.

He was just who she'd hoped he would be.

Helen had done her research. High-end collectibles were a specialized business, and there were only a handful of dealers in the Bay Area who carried the right sort of inventory. She'd been retired for ten years, but her contacts were still varied and reliable. After carefully considering the information they'd provided, she had decided Martin Blake might be just the man to act as her—executor.

His shop was tasteful enough, and his online auctions brought high-end buyers from around the world. But what had gotten him from a squalid secondhand book-shop in the Tenderloin to this more prestigious location was a very lucrative business dealing with a friend of hers. Blake had slicked him out of a sizable collection, apprais-ing it at a fraction of its actual value, buying treasure at thrift-store prices.

Nothing actionable, nothing ever made public. Martin Blake's veneer of respectability had remained intact—if one did not shine too bright a light.

She slowly removed the box, setting it so gently onto the table that there was no sound. For the second time, Helen undid the cords that held the corners of the silk and let it fall away.

She was gratified to hear a sudden, inhaled gasp.

A gleaming shallow case of dark, polished wood, about ten by fifteen inches, lay among the folds of silk, its top framing a sheet of thick glass. Inside was a painting—done in vibrant pastel chalks—on a sheet of heavy art paper.

Martin Blake did an almost comic double take. His eyes widened, his mouth hung open. "Is that—?"

"Haskel's last painting."

The illustration showed a slender, russet-haired young man in evening clothes, dancing with a woman in a shimmering blue jumpsuit that clung to every curve, her hair a sleek blond waterfall. They gazed into each other's eyes with obvious joy. The dancers stood in a skylit library. Behind them, a wall of windows revealed the skyline of the city and the expanse of the bay spread out below.

In the bottom right-hand corner was the familiar, angular signature.

"Jesus," said Martin Blake.

"Indeed," Helen replied dryly. She allowed him to gawp for a full ten minutes in silence. He circled the table slowly, looking at the painting from every angle. He squatted down, peering across its surface, then went to his desk and returned with a pair of white cotton gloves and a large magnifying glass. He scrutinized the signature, then the box itself, running a finger along the edges of the glass, the smooth, unmarked wooden sides.

"How do I open it?" he asked finally.

"You don't. It's sealed. Watertight and— nearly—airtight."

He sputtered. "How am I supposed to examine the painting?"

"Are you interested in purchasing it?"

"If it can be authenticated, I would consider making an offer." His face held a curious mixture of emotions, those of a man whose dreams have just come true and who cannot believe it. He looked simultaneously ecstatic and poleaxed.

"I'm sure I can answer any questions," Helen said.

He touched the case again, stroking it, and she watched his eyes shift—a slyer, more calculating look now.

"I have my doubts," he said after a moment. "It's not his usual subject matter. There's no menace. It looks like the cover for a romance title, and Haskel never worked for those houses." He tented his fingers under his chin. "There's no space for a title, and I'm even more troubled by the setting—the details of the room and the city beyond. That's not his style at all. Haskel's *figures* were elaborate and explicit, but his backgrounds were notably bare, nearly abstract." He gestured to the cover of the magazine lying in its tray.

"All true," Helen said.

"Still, it's an interesting piece." He circled the table again, his steps firmer now. In control. About to make a deal. Helen amused herself watching him evaluate the situation. He *wanted* it, she knew, as much as he'd ever wanted anything in his life. Just how cunning would he try to be?

He stopped and placed his hands on the table. "Tell you what," he said with a weasely smile. "I'm a gambling man. I'll give you twenty thousand for it."

"Really?" Helen did not return the smile. "I seem to remember you saying the last Haskel went for three times that at auction. And that this," she touched the box, "was—what did you call it? Ah, yes. The Holy Grail. Try again."

Blake paled. He straightened up, jamming his hands into his pockets. Helen noticed that his palms had left faint damp spots on the polished wood.

She had him.

"That painting was sold by a reputable auction house, and came with indisputable provenance," he said, his words clipped. "You certainly can't expect me to just take your *word* for this."

"Of course not," Helen said. She pulled a black-and-white photo and a scrap of paper from the pocket of her jacket. "I was there when it was painted. Here's your provenance." She handed it to him.

The photo was small, less than three inches square, with a thin border and deckled edges. In it, the painting lay on a drafting table, a work-in-progress; the background was half done, the figures lightly sketched in. A hand holding a piece of chalk was just visible at the left edge. Off to one side, the boy in the painting, in shirtsleeves and trousers, one knee drawn up, sat perched on a windowsill. Next to him stood a slim Asian girl in an embroidered cream jacket.

The paper held two handwritten words: *Thanks.
—Haskel*

"Provenance enough?"

He stared. "You're saying that's *you* watching him work?"

"It is." She plucked at her lapels. "Same jacket."

"When was this taken?"

Helen turned the snapshot over. On the back, written in pencil, was a date: September 17, 1940.

"Sorry. I don't buy it. That's got to be your mother."

"It's not." She watched him try and do the math, could almost see the wheels turning as he counted.

"No way. You'd have to be, like—a hundred years old."

"I am. Would you like to see my ID?" She gave him her most judiciary stare.

"I—I suppose not." He frowned. "But even if that *is* you, I would never buy a piece without examining it."

"Examine away."

"I mean close up. Out of the case."

Helen smiled. It was not the sort of smile anyone would want to see twice. "Once our transaction is complete, you are welcome to take any action you choose. But I caution you. The painting, as you can see, was done in chalk pastels. You just explained how fragile a medium that is." She tapped the side of the box, a sharp knuckle rap, and watched as a few powdery grains shifted on the surface.

"Jesus. Don't!"

"*That* is why it was sealed. It can be lifted—carefully—but not shaken or disturbed, as you just saw."

"Other original Haskels have survived."

"Fixative," Helen said, the **F** so firm it almost popped in her mouth.

He snorted. "Well, of course."

"Not this one."

He stared, at her, at the painting. "Impossible. Not in that condition."

"It has been stored under—optimal—circumstances."

He circled the table again. "No one else has seen this?" he asked after several minutes.

"I give you my word, no other living soul knows about *this* painting." She gave a small shrug. "I do have an appointment later today with another buyer, if you decline." She named the man and watched Blake's jaw clench. "All I've told him is that it's an original Haskel."

Beads of sweat appeared on his forehead. The photograph in his hand trembled. He noticed her glance and put it down next to the wooden case.

"How much?" he finally asked. His voice cracked like an adolescent's.

"Two hundred thousand," Helen said, as if it were a casual figure. "Wired to my account. Here's the bill of sale." She pulled a sheet of paper from her pocket and laid it on the table. She had called in a few final favors, and knew, to the penny, what funds he had. He could cover it, but only just. "You will not get another chance, Mr. Blake."

The blood drained from his face, his absurd goatee dark against pale flesh tinged a sickly grayish green. He had the sort of expression so common to *Weird Menace* covers, a deer caught in the most horrible of headlights. It was, she thought, an exquisite dilemma, pitting his greed against his better judgment. He knew it was the find of a lifetime, a legendary piece, one that would elevate him to the most exclusive circles in his field. But—

Martin Blake stared at the wooden case for five minutes without seeming to breathe. Helen waited. She was a very patient woman.

Finally he picked up the document. His lips moved slightly as he read. It was half a page, transferring the painting to him, with its current condition agreed upon by both parties. With a few lines of legalese, it also relieved her, upon his signature, of any liability, responsibility, or future claims regarding the work.

"That's it?" he asked.

"It is. When my banker has confirmed the transfer, we sign and the painting is yours."

Fifteen minutes later, Helen said, "Yes. Thank you so much," pushed END CALL, and slipped her phone into her pocket. She folded the silk and the Neiman Marcus bag under one arm, and shook Martin Blake's hand. "Congratulations," she said, retrieving her cane. "It's a *very* special painting."

Blake could only nod. He walked her to the front of the store and held the door as she exited onto Geary Street, the bell jingling faintly behind her.

Caveat emptor, she thought, and turned toward Union Square.

Four

Helen walked slowly, but with a spring in her step. Her first stop was her bank, where she withdrew the transferred funds and closed the account. She gave the clerk the addresses of the GLBT Historical Society, the San Francisco Art Institute, and the friend who had been swindled. "Fifty thousand to each of those. Cashier's checks, please."

Martin Blake would be utterly baffled, but Haskel, she thought, would have approved.

The remainder she took in cash, five banded stacks of hundred-dollar bills. She asked the bank manager to call a cab, and went home. Her phone buzzed as she was finishing lunch. The caller ID said: Blake. She let it go to voice mail. When he called again, two minutes later, she turned off the phone and went to take a nap.

The next morning, she hired a Cadillac convertible and a driver for one last day in the city that she loved. To Chinatown for tea and almond cookies, Fisherman's Wharf for a lunch of Dungeness crab and champagne. In the afternoon, she went to North Beach and Russian Hill, visiting the places she had first discovered when she'd moved to San Francisco at the age of nineteen, the places where she and Haskel had become friends. Never *more* than that, although Helen had once entertained hopes they— She sighed. Water under a long-closed bridge.

Some of the landmarks of her memories were gone—the Monkey Block had been torn down more than fifty years before, to make way for the Transamerica Pyramid; 440 Broadway remained a seedy bar, but with a very different clientele than Mona's. Only Lupo's seemed the same, secure in its old location, even if the sign said Tommaso's; its pizza was still delicious and its red wine robust—for twenty-first-century prices, of course.

Each place she stopped to eat or drink, she left a sizable tip for the startled waiter or waitress—ten thousand dollars in cash. The astonished smiles and tears were the finest part of a very fine day. By the time the driver took her back to her building, it was evening. He held the car door, shocked when she handed him the fifth stack of bills.

"Thank you for a lovely day," she said, tapping her cane on the sidewalk. "I will remember it for the rest of my life."

She went upstairs, weary but content. Every box on her To-Do list had been ticked off, one by one. Her realtor would sell the building on Spofford Alley. She had no children, and had outlived most of her friends, so her lawyer had drawn up a will with a generous bequest to Ivy, her caregiver, and a smaller one to her attentive doorman. The remainder of her estate she left to the Manzanar Committee, along with a few trusts and gifts to various charities. All done and dusted.

Most important, she had kept her oath, and seen to Haskel's painting. Seventy-five years. She smiled.

It was time.

Her keys and wallet centered on the kitchen counter where Ivy would be sure to see them in the morning, she poured the last of the Macallan into a tall tumbler. She walked to the big window and stood for a minute, quietly gazing at the city spread out below her, the canyons of tall buildings spotted here and there with traffic signals and the yellow glow of sodium lamps, the ever-changing pattern of lights on the new Bay Bridge flickering off to the east.

Then she opened the bottle of pills, and took them, two at a time, with a swallow of good scotch until there was nothing left of either.

Helen Young went into her bedroom. She changed into a pair of blue silk pajamas, brushed her hair, and put on a touch of lipstick. Then she got into bed, turned out the light, and went to sleep for the last time, humming a Cole Porter tune until she and the melody simply drifted away.

PARTY TRICKS

PARTY TRICKS

From a tiny room in the midst of the bustle of Chinatown, low snippets of conversation—in English—wafted out to the cracked pavement though a half-open door. Franny Travers bent over a wooden table, pale oak topped with a sheet of cobalt glass. A teapot on a bamboo tray anchored one corner, a sheaf of closely typed papers another.

"Sign there, there, and there. Initial there, sign *there*, and it's done," her companion said. She was a young Asian woman in a fashionable suit from the City of Paris—pencil skirt, high-necked blouse, peplum jacket. Her ink-black hair was perfectly coifed—finger-rolled and lacquered—her red lipstick flawless, her skin a warm ivory.

Franny uncapped her fountain pen. A small woman in her mid-forties, she wore her dark hair in a blunt cut—part Dutch boy, part flapper's bob—and sported a jade tunic over a pair of loose black trousers. "Why is it so complicated?"

"You're a woman. You own two buildings. And you've written a will leaving them to your live-in *friend*. None of

that sits easy with the courts." She tapped one of the papers. "That's why I've spent the last three weeks making
sure it's unbreakable. *Every single i* is dotted, *t*'s crossed,
all the *heretofores* and *in perpetuities*—and blab, blab,
blab."

"That's why you're the lawyer."

"Almost a year now," Helen Young said. "Though
you're still one of my only clients. Unlike the stuffed
white shirts downtown, you don't seem to mind being
represented by the yellow peril." She made a face. "And
no one around *here* is willing to take advice about money
from a mere woman."

"I like to keep my business 'in the life' when I can."
Franny scrawled her name with a flourish and capped her
pen. "How *do* you make ends meet?"

Helen shrugged. "Fifteen years of ballet and tap classes
trumps three of law school. If I weren't dancing twelve
shows a week at Forbidden City, I'd've had to hock this
suit long ago." She smiled. "Letting me live here rent-free
is a very generous fee. I can't tell you how much that'll
help."

"I'm glad." Franny fitted a Lucky Strike into a jade
holder and lit it, blowing the smoke in the direction of
the doorway. "Your apartment is painted and furnished,
but there'll be noisy workmen in the other five for a
month at least."

"I'll cope. When are you going to advertise them?"

"I'm not. The world is at war—even if we seem to have the luxury of pretending otherwise—and I have European friends desperate to get people out. The refugees will need places to stay, away from prying eyes."

"Chinatown fits the bill."

"It does," she agreed. "And where else can you get dried toads?"

Helen laughed, then looked at the thin, faux-gold watch on her wrist. "It's almost six. Isn't tonight your little salon?"

"The Circle!" Franny swore. "I forgot. They'll be ringing my bell in fifteen minutes. At least Babs is handling dinner."

Helen glanced down at her T-strap heels. "I brought the papers straight from the clerk's office, but it's a good mile to Russian Hill, most of it fairly steep. I'll never make it in these shoes. We'll have to flag a cab."

"In Chinatown?" Franny snorted. "Besides, taxis always have difficulty finding my house." She drummed her fingers on the glass for a moment, flipping a mental coin. "Just this once," she said aloud.

Franny reached into a drawer and removed a hand-painted map the size of a cocktail napkin. She folded it, her fingers moving too fast for Helen to follow, burnishing each crease with the edge of a pale bone knife until a little envelope no bigger than a saltine lay in her palm.

"How will that help?"

"By creating a temporary rearrangement of the available space. A short cut." She put it into the pocket of her trousers. "It's a—hobby—of mine."

They walked to the end of the alley and turned right into a shaded lane. Houses lined one side, facing a high rock-walled garden.

"What the *hell* just happened?" Helen asked, her voice loud with surprise. "That wasn't a *mile*. And there was no hill at all."

"Oh, there was. Is." Franny said vaguely. "San Francisco is a city well-suited to magic." She unfolded the paper and placed it in a soot-tarnished brass bowl on her doorstep. Striking a match, she lit one corner and watched it crumble to ash. "There. All back in place again."

"What the—?"

"It's complicated." Franny held the door open. "Let's have a drink, shall we?

"Sure." Helen looked back at the street with a bewildered expression. "I think I need one."

The house had irregular brickwork and a bay window below a copper-domed cupola. They stepped into a hallway, white walls full of colorful art, a staircase rising on the right.

Helen smiled when they reached the archway that opened onto the second floor, one large, airy space with a kitchen and small table at the near end, and low green armchairs and a couch grouped around a rug at the other. Between them a spiral staircase helixed up next to a library table covered with books and maps. Paper sculptures in bright colors dotted the overflowing bookshelves.

"I love this room," she said. "Is that new *ori-kami*?"

Franny raised an eyebrow. "It's not a well-known art in this country."

"My grandmother folded animals for me when I was little."

"Ah."

Facing north, a wall of atelier windows, reminiscent of Paris, angled in to the ceiling. Seven wide panes spanned the width of the room, thin dividers painted the green of young spinach. Beyond the glass lay the city. Ziggurats of stone walls and white houses cascaded vertically down to the bay and Alcatraz and the blue-distant hills.

Two walls were covered, floor-to-ceiling, with a hodgepodge of books: crumbling leather-bound tomes—many of them in languages Helen did not recognize; technical books and treatises on cartography, mathematics, and alchemy; a scattering of modern best sellers; and heavy, illustrated volumes on art from antiquity to Bauhaus.

Franny laid out the drinks cart while Helen perused

the shelves and, as always, admired the view. The front door opened, followed by the soft tread of footsteps. A woman with short, honey-colored hair and tortoiseshell spectacles appeared, wearing a skirt and sweater and carrying two flat cardboard boxes, envelopes and magazines stacked on top of them.

"You got your mail, Babs?" Franny kissed the woman on the cheek.

"I stopped by Terry's after class." She set the boxes down on the kitchen table. "And picked up two pies from Lupo's. I'll slide them into the oven to keep warm. Hello, Helen. You look quite spiffy today."

"Thanks," Helen replied. "Why don't they just drop your mail through the slot?"

"I use my sister's house as my 'official' address. If the university found out about Franny and me, I'd be out on my ear."

"The risks of being a professor."

"I wish. I'm still just a mathematics lecturer. Seems my Ph.D. is less significant than my ovaries. This semester I have one class of bonehead algebra, and I'm training some aspiring computers to use slide rules and logarithmic tables."

"Fun stuff."

"It has its moments." Babs removed lettuce, green onions, a carrot, and an alligator pear from the refrigerator. "Pop a bottle of the Chianti, Fran?"

"Just did. And opened the bourbon. Haskel will want a cocktail."

"Truer words." She turned to Helen. "Name your poison."

"Beer, please." She draped her suit jacket over the back of a chair. "Mind if I kick these heels off? My dogs are killing me."

"Make yourself comfortable." Franny set about clearing the library table, laying out five woven mats and matching napkins. Babs added a cruet of oil and vinegar and a wooden bowl brimming with greens and chopped vegetables.

"It's open," Franny called at the sound of a knock.

"I see," said a voice from below. This woman was close to six feet in flat shoes, broad-shouldered and long-legged. Her hair was a deep blond, pulled back and fastened with a silvery clip at the nape of her neck. She wore khaki slacks, a white shirt dusted with smudges of color, and a simple blue pendant. She brushed at a smear of crimson on her rolled-up sleeve. "Sorry," she said in a low, throaty voice. "I was working on a painting and didn't have time to change." She set a paper sack on the table.

Franny smiled. "You know the Circle is come as you are, Haskel. Drink?"

"Please. Hi, Helen." She accepted a squat tumbler of

amber whiskey, and lit a cigarette, the first of many. "Do I smell Lupo's?"

"You do. One cheese and olives, one prosciutto and peppers."

"My family is baffled that I eat *pie* for dinner," Helen said. "I tell them it's a neighborhood specialty, but they still think it's queer."

"It certainly is tonight." Franny laughed. She turned toward the kitchen. "In ten minutes I'm going to take the *pizzas* out before they turn into roof tiles. I hope our last guest can find the place."

"Who is it?"

"A delightful young thing I found at Mona's."

Everyone was helping herself to a second drink when another knock sounded.

"It's open."

A moment later, a slender, athletic woman bounded up the stairs, two at a time, and stood in the archway, slightly breathless. She had short, curly auburn hair, freckles, and a crooked grin. Dressed in dungarees and a plaid cotton shirt, she could easily have been mistaken for a boy.

"Sorry if I'm late. I got rather lost," she said with the plummy, slightly clipped intonation of a New England blue blood. "Something smells delicious."

Franny slid the flat, fragrant tomato pies onto a platter

and began cutting each of them into eight wedges. "It does. You're just in time to eat." She gestured around the room. "First, let me make introductions. Emily Netterfield, meet my partner-in-crime, Barbara Weiss. Babs. Helen Young, my attorney. And my dear friend, Loretta Haskel."

"Just Haskel is fine."

"We met years ago in the library at the Art Institute," Franny said. "I was researching pigments—"

"—and I was looking at naughty pictures."

"For fun or profit?" Emily asked. She accepted a glass of wine and sat in the nearest chair.

"Both. I'm a painter. And I like naked women."

Babs smiled. "Don't we all?" She took a seat at the end of the table.

"Have I seen your work?" Emily asked.

"It depends. Do you read *Weird Menace*?"

"That penny dreadful? No, can't say as I do."

"Then probably not." Haskel stubbed out her cigarette and sat down with the others.

They ate and conversed, passing the salad and the slices of pie. They were all old friends, and Emily felt a little out of place. They weren't excluding her, but she knew none of the people or events they discussed. She'd been surprised at the invitation to this dinner party, unsure why she'd accepted. Perhaps because Franny had seemed like a cultured, educated—and like-minded—woman, and she longed for that connection. She'd been in the city more than a year, but had found it hard to make new friends.

She'd gone to girls' schools, assumed she'd be a spinster English teacher like Miss Schaefer. That changed in her junior year at Wellesley, when she'd met Jilly. Fast friends, and then more, and then true love. Capital **T**, capital **L**. They planned to get an apartment together after graduation, live like Bohemians, gloriously free.

But a nosy proctor sent their lives down the rabbit hole. They shared a room, as girls do, and a bed, as *nice* girls do not. Both were expelled. No time to say goodbye. She was packing when Jilly's parents came to drive her to the country "for a rest." A lovely place with green lawns and locked doors and treatments to help Jilly become a suitable wife for the understanding husband they would provide.

Typewriter in one hand, suitcase in the other, Emily boarded a westbound train before her own parents had the chance to decide *her* future. She stared without seeing as the country rolled by, no life, no plans. Three days later, she was in San Francisco.

"—don't you?"

Emily started. Franny was looking at her. "Sorry," she said. "Woolgathering. It's the wine. Goes straight to my head." She felt herself redden and changed the subject.

"That's a lovely necklace," she said to Haskel, across the table. "What sort of stone is it?" It was an irregular, pale blue oval that flashed a deep indigo in the right light.

"I don't know. It's from the old country. When I graduated from high school, my bubbe gave it to me, along with her recipe for *tundérpör* and a bus ticket out of Pittsburgh. Told me it will help me escape trouble if I always wear it."

"Do you?"

"Why tempt fate?"

Emily helped herself to another slice of pie. "I'm afraid I don't believe in that kind of supernatural baloney."

"Supernatural, perhaps. Baloney, perhaps not." Franny fitted a cigarette into her jade holder. "Do you believe in luck?"

"Well, I—"

"There. You see. Rabbit's foot, four-leaf clover. Everyone makes some exceptions." She patted Babs's hand. "Even my logical, pragmatic friend here put a mezuzah on the front door."

Helen looked up. "That's religion, not magic."

"Is there a difference?" Franny asked. "Don't science, magic, and religion all claim to reveal worlds of mystery and unexpected possibilities?"

"Here we go," Babs said with a smile. "Franny's hobbyhorse."

"What if the 'supernatural' is just—" Franny continued, "—the odds and ends we don't yet know how to label?"

"Franny's certainly got talents *I* can't explain," said Helen. She lowered her voice to a whisper. "I think she's a, a—" she stammered, groping for a word. "A witch."

"That is an ugly, prejudicial term." Franny made a face. "Like dike."

Helen nodded. "Or Chink. Sorry. I get it. But you must be *some* kind of—?"

"In essence, yes." Franny sighed and turned to Emily, who was chuckling. "You're a skeptic. You don't believe in powerful, invisible forces?"

"Certainly not."

"Radio waves? Magnetism?"

"That's different."

"Is it? How about mysteriously glowing deadly rocks?" Franny smiled. "Oh, right. Radium is *science*."

Emily shook her head. "Now you're confusing apples and oranges."

"Really? I find apples often turn out to *be* oranges." She stubbed out her cigarette and produced a hand-rolled one in a second holder of black jet. "The green one is only for tobacco," she explained. She lit the end, drew the smoke in, and handed it to Helen.

"Think about, oh—germs," Franny said, exhaling

slowly. "That's proper science now, but in the past, sickness *was* linked to witchcraft, the devil. *Woo-oo-ooo.*" She made a spooky noise. "Even fifty years ago—modern times the very idea that tiny, tiny animals were the cause of disease got some doctors laughed out of the academy."

Helen turned to Babs. "You're the scientific sort. What do you think of all this?"

"I have to admit, I've seen Franny do things that can't be understood logically." She took a drag on the reefer, passed it on to Haskel. "Although I'm making headway. My dissertation was on topology, rubber-sheet geometry—the properties of a surface that don't change when it's stretched or twisted."

"Or folded," Franny added.

"Yes." She thought for a moment. "I'll give you a demonstration." She got up, carrying a pile of plates to the kitchen, and returned with a second bottle of wine and a long strip of paper. She made a dot on one side, labeling it **A**, turned the paper over and made another dot, **B**. "Two points, one on the front, one on the back, right? No way to connect them."

Everyone nodded.

"Okay." She twisted the strip and fastened the loose ends with a paper clip. "How about now?"

"Still one dot on each side," Emily said with confidence. This was a very odd party.

"Are you sure?"

"I've dealt with paper before. Always has two sides."

"Okay. Let's test that hypothesis. Haskel, you're good with a pencil. See if you can connect the dots."

"My hand's a little wobbly at the moment, but I'll try," Haskel said. She laid the paper on the table and touched the pencil to the **A**. She slowly drew a line down the narrow strip, pulling the paper along, the pencil never leaving the surface, until its tip touched the **B**. "Like that?"

Emily stared. "How on earth—?"

"It's called a Mobius strip," Babs said. "After the twist, it only has *one* side."

Helen whistled. "Pretty slick. Is that how Franny's little short cuts work?"

"What short cuts?" Emily asked.

"I'm a cartographer. Under the right circumstances, I can create maps that, when folded precisely, form unexpected pathways."

"You're joking."

"She's not," Babs said. "And yes, Helen, I think it is, at least in theory. I've seen those short cuts. Since anything observable can be described mathematically, they should be reproducible."

"How's that going?" Haskel said.

"I'm stuck in some fairly key places."

Franny patted her hand. "It's *magic,* darling. Some bits are beyond the laws of logic." She stopped for a moment. "Hmm. No—magic does—must—obey its own laws, they just can't be expressed in your terms."

"*Yet,*" Babs said. "The *ori-kami* folding is mathematically elegant and topologically fascinating. So is cartographic theory. But merely combining the two has no effect. That's where I'm flummoxed. Franny does something—else—that transforms space and time."

"Time?" Franny looked startled. "Oh. I hadn't—I suppose so, which means—" she put down her napkin and got up. "Forgive my rudeness, but I *must* make a few notes. Carry on. This is a *most* scintillating group."

Babs twiddled the paper loop. "Trying to quantify Franny's work may be a wild goose chase, but that's how mathematical breakthroughs happen—trying to describe the indescribable. Finding the pattern no one else has noticed."

"I'd call that creativity," Haskel said, nodding. "It's not rational either, not—pin-down-able."

"Yep. There's as much art to science as there is science to art."

"I'll buy that. Light and shadow, perspective. I don't pretend to understand the physics or geometry, but I couldn't paint without them."

"Don't forget the magic words," Emily said, a note of

mockery in her voice. She felt very peculiar. She didn't smoke, but the air was quite fragrant, and she was no longer sure *what* she believed.

"I can't forget them," Haskel said. "When I said, 'I do' ten years ago, it certainly changed *my* world."

"You're *married*?" Emily had assumed everyone at the table was, well—like her. She felt an odd surge of disappointment, which was ridiculous. She had no interest at all in this calm, gray-eyed painter. None. She poured herself more wine.

"Me too," said Helen. "It's convenient. Eddie—my dance partner—is a nance. He needed the respectability, and marrying a white girl is illegal so—" She shrugged. "Besides, I like his last name. Mine was too long to fit on a marquee."

"What was it?" Babs asked.

"Yamaguchi."

"You're Japanese?"

"No, just American. Born and raised in Coos Bay, Oregon. So was my dad, and my grandfather. I don't speak the language, I don't know much about the culture. I just *look* foreign." She patted her own cheek. "Other than this mug of mine, I'm as much Japanese as you are, what—German? Everyone has ancestors."

"My mother's people came over on the *Mayflower*," Emily said. Conversation stopped. The others looked at her. Flustered, she said quickly, "Why *pretend* to be Chinese?"

"I don't. Well, except at work, but so do half the other performers— Korean, Filipino, Chinese, Japanese—the tourists can't tell the difference. To them we're all just mysterious Orientals."

"Ah. Speaking of which," Haskel said. "I have something for you." She opened the paper sack and took out two magazines, their unbound edges ragged, rough as slices of raw tree. The vivid cover of *Weird Menace* showed a naked woman, her breasts barely concealed by a spill of blond hair, fleeing from a swarm of tiny winged demons. *Diabolical Dr. Wu Yang* featured another scantily clad woman in peril, this one threatened on one side by a lobsterish creature and on the other by a sinister-looking man in Chinese robes, his talon-like nails reaching for her throat. CLAWS OF THE YELLOW LEGION was printed beneath the image.

"Ugh," Emily said. "Those are almost—pornographic."

"I didn't even know Haskel owned a pornograph," Helen said, reaching for the second magazine. "I turned out pretty good." She laughed when Babs raised an eyebrow. "Didn't I mention that I model for Haskel from time to time?"

"When I need an Oriental villain."

"Aren't they all, in your line of work?" Babs asked.

"Yes. And all scientists are evil, busy inventing death rays or breeding monsters."

"Everyone needs a hobby. Fran, have you seen my death ray?"

"It's in the cupboard, with the clean linens," Franny said, returning to the table. "Now, who's ready for dessert?"

FORBIDDEN LOVE

"Hold the knife out a little more." Haskel peered into the viewfinder of her camera. "Look menacing."

Helen raised her arm, gravity tugging against the wide sleeve of the heavy, embroidered robe. "And inscrutable?"

"Of course." Haskel steadied the camera. "That's it. Hold it." She took a shot, wound the film forward quickly, took three more. "Good. I can work from these."

"Finally." Helen let her arm drop to her side, the prop knife dangling. "I like playing dress-up, but Dr. Wu Yang needs some summer-weight clothes."

"You're the one raiding the costume department." Haskel put down the camera and sketched a few quick charcoal lines onto a pad of paper.

"Mine are all on the skimpy side."

"Next time you can be the terrified victim." Haskel lit a cigarette and leaned against a worktable covered with pastel chalks, jars of paintbrushes and pencils. "But Oriental fiends are harder to find."

"That's a relief."

"I suppose."

Helen took off the round black silk cap with its red tasseled topknot and opened the robe. The breeze from the open window played across her damp skin.

Haskel's studio was two rooms on the top floor of the Montgomery Block, a squat brown building built in the mid-1800s whose massive bulk surrounded an inner courtyard, filling the interior with natural light. Each room had two windows and a skylight whose slanted glass roof caught the rose-gold glow of both sunset and dawn. The floor was planked wood, knobbed with drips of paint from nine decades of easels.

"Do me one more favor?" Haskel asked.

"Probably."

"Raid Fish Alley one night after work? I'm almost out of fixative."

"Sure. Heads and bones do? Sturgeon bladders have been scarce. The fishmongers sell them for soup."

"Whatever you can scrounge."

"I'll do what I can." Helen let the robe slide to the floor and stood in her bra and slip. She raised her arms over her head, stretching her shoulders, then reached for her toes, her body bent 180 degrees. "Do me a favor back?"

"What?"

"Leering and menacing made me thirsty."

"I have bourbon."

"I know." Helen grimaced. "Let's walk over to Mona's and have a proper cocktail."

"Alright. I haven't been there since they moved."

"That was last year."

"I don't go out much." She looked down at her coveralls. "Give me a minute to change while you dress."

The neighborhood around her building had been fashionable at one time, but at the end of the Depression it verged on the unkempt, squalid in the shadows. Rents were cheap; nearly every building housed artists, writers, actors, and musicians.

Mona's Club 440 was three blocks up Montgomery Street and a block to the left, at the seedy end of Broadway, an even tougher quarter that stayed in business largely for the purpose of shocking tourists. Visitors who'd come to San Francisco for the world's fair ventured nervously into the city at night to gape at curiosities that would astound the guys at the office, the ladies in the bridge club back in Dubuque or Chattanooga.

Mona's occupied the ground floor of a nondescript three-story building, fire escapes zigzagging up the stucco facade. Above an awning hung a metal sign spelling out the name in bright neon, coloring the sidewalk below with garish light.

The club was many things to many people. A tourist trap. A neighborhood bar. A haven where women who loved each other could meet in public without fear or the shame of sidelong glances from "nice" ladies. Mona took care of her girls—butches, femmes, Flos, Freddies, wanna-bees, looky-loos, he-shes. At Mona's, a girl could be anyone she dreamed, even if for just one night, no questions asked. Or at least no answers required.

Inside, a long bar lined the left wall, a hat-check nook at its far end. An archway led into the show room, with a line of booths down one wall and tables around the stage at the front.

The place was crowded when Helen and Haskel walked in. There were tourists galore, and dozens of women: in dresses and makeup; in slacks and blouses; in rough work clothes, their hair cut short; in tailored men's suits, hair slicked back with brilliantine, like movie stars. There was a *world* of difference between Clark Gable and Wallace Beery, Haskel thought as she made her way to the bar, waving in passing to a few artists she knew.

"I swear, Edna. That one *has* to be a man," said a middle-aged woman in a flowery dress. She held on to her glass of beer with both hands, as if it would be snatched at any moment.

"No, Irene. I told you, it's like the ad in the theater program promised—Mona's. Where girls will be boys."

"Well, I don't believe it," the florid woman said. "It's just not natural." The two of them headed toward the show room.

"Tonight they come to see us, tomorrow they'll drive

out to the zoo and stare at the monkeys." The woman tending bar straightened her bow tie. "What'll it be?"

"Bourbon, rocks." Haskel turned to Helen. "What are you drinking?"

"Gin and tonic, thanks."

"Coming up." The bartender reached around for a glass. "Shouldn't complain, I guess. It's dough from rubes like that keeps us in business, keeps the cops off our backs."

Haskel tasted her drink. "How do you figure?"

"If it was just *us*, they'd close the place in a heartbeat. What we are is against the law, you know."

"So I've heard." She handed Helen her drink.

"But the city needs tourists. And *they* want a peek at the down-and-dirty. Tell the folks back home they saw honest-to-god perverts."

"Do you get much trouble?"

"Now and then. Usually late, when drunk guys need to prove something—'what you want is a *real* man, baby,'" she said in a gruff voice. She polished a glass and set it on the back bar. "I can usually spot 'em. I start watering their drinks—and charging them double. They hightail it somewhere else, muttering about decency."

"Figures." Haskel laid a dollar on the bar.

A piano sat at the foot of the stage, a burly crop-haired woman in a pinstriped suit expertly playing casual music as the place filled up. A glass of whiskey and a fishbowl sat on the back of the upright, the bottom of the bowl covered with loose change, a dollar bill resting on it like flotsam.

The booths were full. Helen spotted a small, round table two rows back, and they settled in with their drinks. Ten minutes later, the lights dimmed, and a spotlight lit the stage.

A slim woman in a white dinner jacket stepped up to the microphone. "Welcome, ladies and gentlemen and—" she winked "—everyone in between." The audience laughed, equal parts amusement and nervous uncertainty.

"Tonight you'll hear songs in English, French—and double entendre." Chuckles from some of the audience, and whispered "What's that?" from a few tables. "First up tonight, singing songs your mother *didn't* teach you, please welcome—Mickey Minton!"

Another spot followed a dapper woman in a tuxedo, her blond hair gelled into a pompadour. The piano player began an up-tempo melody as she stepped to the mike and began to sing a jaunty tune:

"At Mona's Club on old Broadway
You'll hear some people pass and say,
'If you go in there, you'll be surprised:
The boys are girlies in disguise!'"

She paused, waiting for the audience reaction, smiled, and continued.

"But never falter, never fear,
We're here to give the patrons cheer.
You'll never fall and you'll never flub
When you come to *Mona's* Club!"

The audience applauded, Haskel politely, but briefly.

"Not your style?" Helen asked. She signaled a tuxedoed waitress for another drink when the girl replaced the one on the piano.

"Not really. I'm more of a classical gal." Haskel was quiet for a moment. "I suppose I find it odd, parading private lives in public."

"At least we're visible here. We have to hide everywhere else."

"We can only be ourselves as long as we're *entertainment*?" She frowned and lit a cigarette. "I'm not certain that's a good trade-off."

"That's because you can pass, if you want. You dress up and do your hair, you can have tea at the City of Paris. No one would be the wiser. Gals like Big Jack—the piano player—don't have that luxury. Mona's is it."

"She chooses her suits and ties."

"Didn't choose who she *is*." Helen stared at her drink,

then said, quietly, "A lot of places in this town won't even let *me* in the door, no matter how nice I look."

"That's different."

"Is it?"

"No," Haskel said after an uneasy minute. "I don't suppose it is. I hadn't given it much—"

She was interrupted by an arpeggio from Big Jack, signaling the next act. "Butch" Lewis was a squat, tough-looking woman whose shoulders strained her jacket, and whose lyrics danced along the borders of obscenity. "I stole this one from Finocchio's. It's written for a pansy, but hey, queer is queer." She grinned and began a tango-esque version of "I'd Rather Be Spanish Than Mannish."

Then she took the mike off the stand, draped it over one shoulder, and stepped down into the audience as she launched into another ribald ditty. She knelt beside the table of an obvious tourist couple. The man looked, then looked away. The woman giggled and covered her mouth.

The singer moved on to a table where an older man with a pencil-thin moustache sat with his arm slung over the shoulders of a rouged peroxide blonde with a plunging neckline. Butch knelt down.

"This what you want?" the blonde asked, laughing. She lifted up her long, flared skirt, and tented it over the singer's head.

Through the mike, the audience heard a snort of surprise, then a chuckle, and the song shifted to a husky rendition of *"I'll be seeing you—in all the old familiar places—"*

That had the audience in stitches for a good five minutes.

When Butch was done and Big Jack's drink had been replenished again, Haskel stood. "I'm going to use the—"

"—little girls' room?"

"Around here, you can never be sure." She walked to the back corner, disappearing down a narrow hallway. She was rinsing her hands at the sink when she heard a roar from the show room. She stepped back into the hall. The lights had been dimmed, low enough that she had to step carefully to make it back to her table.

"What's the to-do?" she asked.

"Spike, of course. She's why half the room is here—provincials *and* natives."

Haskel finished her drink and looked around for a waitress. "Who's Spike? Another mannish one?"

"More boyish, wouldn't you say?"

"Don't know. Haven't seen her."

Helen stared at her, then laughed. "My god, you have no idea. This will be fun."

Before Haskel had a chance to reply, a single, pinpoint spot illuminated the microphone. A saxophone began a slow, blues-tinged melody that sounded like the city at night: cold drinks and hot neon and people out looking for love, or danger—or both.

A few bars in, a young woman stepped out of the darkness. She wore high-waisted trousers, pleated and cuffed, creased to a knife edge, a fedora cocked at a rakish angle, a few auburn curls straying out. Her white shirt was open at the collar, a cobalt silk scarf at her throat, matching suspenders giving her trim body a streamlined accent. One finger casually hooked a cream-colored dinner jacket over her shoulder. She paused, hip-shot, and grinned out at the audience.

Mona's exploded with noise: applause, whistles, catcalls.

When the cacophony died down a bit, Spike hung the jacket on the back of a chair and turned to the piano player. "I've Got You Under My Skin," she said, and began to sing.

Her voice was smooth and low, an alto that occasionally descended into tenor, like deep, rich honey—relaxed, soft, and intimate. She sang the lyrics as they were written—no parody, no comedy—looking into the middle distance as if she could see the story of the song unfolding.

"Oh, hell!" Haskel gasped in surprise. "That's, that's—what's-her-name. Emily. From Franny's party last month." The snooty, opinionated girl.

Helen nodded. "That's her."

"Jesus." Haskel felt the back of her neck prickle. A smile coaxed itself—uninvited—to the corners of her mouth. "She's *good*," she said when the song was over.

"There's an understatement. Half the women in the room are in love right now. Femmes, mostly, but more than a couple of butches. No one quite knows what to make of her. There'll be a line of stage-door Janies later on, hoping to take her home and make some private magic." She sipped her drink. "Far as I know, no one's ever succeeded. She signs autographs and lets them take all the pictures they want, but that's all."

"How come?"

"Beats me. She could have any woman in San Francisco, but she always goes home solo. Some girls think she's just a snob." She thought for a minute. "I figure either she hasn't met the right girl, or she did—and got her heart broken."

"Usually how it goes."

The next song was another standard, "Tain't Nobody's Business If I Do," almost a cappella, just a few scattered, minor riffs from the piano as accompaniment. Her voice held longing and regret, and a little tinge of anger. Although once again she changed none of the words to adapt it for her audience, it spoke to everyone in the room who'd ever had a secret.

The applause was deafening. Spike stood, head bowed, palms out at her sides, silently acknowledging the acclaim. A bouquet landed at her feet. Women stood and called her name, over and over, like a primitive chant, like an invocation.

Haskel noticed that half her new drink was already gone, and her cheeks were damp. She wiped her face with the cocktail napkin, the faintest tremble in her hand. She didn't cry. Hadn't cried in years, had steeled herself out of the habit.

"Do you take requests?" called a woman from the far wall.

"I can think of a few things *I'd* like," yelled a red-faced man in a checked suit.

Spike ignored him and turned to the booths, her hands in her trouser pockets, and waited. The room quieted.

"'Come Rain or Come Shine'?" the woman asked in an unsteady voice, as if she could not quite believe everything had stopped just for her.

A two-beat, then Spike nodded. "That's a good one." She leaned over the piano. "F-major, but bluesy, okay Jack?"

The big woman shrugged and played a few bars. "Like that?"

"Just so." She stepped back, took the microphone in both hands, and crooned, "*I'm gonna love you, like no-*

body's loved you, come rain—"

When the song ended, the room was silent for a full minute. No one moved, no one clinked a glass or snapped a lighter or whispered to a friend. Spike stood motionless, then replaced the mike on its stand. As she did, she looked up and saw Haskel. Her head stuttered in surprise, as if she'd gotten a shock from a doorknob. She closed her eyes for a fraction of a second, then opened them and looked directly at the second row.

Haskel felt as if the room had disappeared. Nothing but that green-eyed gaze, making her feel as though every cell in her body was straining to pay attention, hold this moment, then run—hard—and bury it somewhere deep so the *need* of it wouldn't scare the living daylights out of her. She bit her lip, the flicker of small pain breaking the spell, and raised her hands in cadenced, slow applause—Clap. Clap. Clap.—until everyone else joined in.

Now half the room was standing, whistling and stomping and calling Spike's name. As before, she stood, palms out, unmoving. But her head was not bowed. She was looking at Haskel with a little half-grin that said, "So. Whad'ya think of *that*?"

The spotlight switched off, leaving the stage in darkness. Jack ran a long, flourishy riff down the keyboard, then stood up and bowed. "Intermission, folks. Half an hour to refill those drinks or make a new friend." She picked up her own drink, and the fishbowl, now brimming with bills, and exited at the back of the stage.

Haskel sat, staring at the Formica tabletop.

"You okay?" Helen asked.

"Why wouldn't I be?" She drained her drink and stubbed out the cigarette that had burned down to a tube of ash. "I think I'll head home." She stood. "You going to stick around?"

"I shouldn't. Eddie wants to rehearse a new routine at noon, and we've got three shows tomorrow night. An early evening wouldn't kill me." They moved slowly through the crush of people heading toward the bar, jostling against the silk, wool, and coarse cotton shoulders of the mixed crowd.

"I tell ya, that last dame was something else," a man in a tweed jacket said. "If she was a *real* woman, she could play in a classy club."

Haskel stopped, patting her pockets. "I left my smokes on the table. You go on ahead, get that beauty rest."

"Okay. I'll bring some fish parts around in a day or two."

"Thanks." When Haskel returned, people were three deep around the bar. She stood near the open front door. On the sidewalk, a woman in a leather jacket leaned against a lamppost, smoking. Big Jack came out the side entrance, drink in hand. "Bum one, Jonesy?"

"Sure." She shook a Camel free from the pack. Jack lit it with a flip of her silver Zippo and blew a cloud of blue smoke into the foggy San Francisco night. At the east end of the street, the colored lights from Treasure Island filled the sky like an aurora, tinting the darkness with pastels.

A tourist couple exited, the man helping his wife into a thin green coat with a fox-fur collar. "Okay, Sue Ann. You've had your fun. Now can we go someplace normal?"

"Not *yet*, Bill," she said in a voice with vowels as flat as the prairie. "There's another show. I wanna hear that piano player again. He was swell."

"I tole you, Sue Ann. There's no *he*'s in this joint. That's just a fat bulldagger, and she don't even play that great, if you ask me."

"Nobody did." Jack shifted the Camel to the side of her mouth and took a step forward.

Jonesy put a hand on Jack's sleeve. "Let it be."

Jack shook her off and took a second step toward the couple.

The man put his arm out. "Keep away from my wife."

"No problem, pal." Jack ground the cigarette out with the toe of one black brogan. "Bony-ass gal," she said, not quite under her breath.

"Ah, for crissakes, Jack," Jonesy pleaded. "Shut your trap." Jack had a temper when she was drunk, and from the looks of it, she was a couple of sheets to the wind already.

Too late.

"Why, you!" The man drew his arm back for a punch; Jack stepped around it, sending a quick right jab to the gut that dropped him like a sack of potatoes.

Sue Ann screamed and bent to one knee. "Bill? Bill, honey?"

At the sound of the scream, three things happened. The bartender flicked the switch under the bar, flashing the lights inside once, warning of the possibility of trouble. A siren sounded a block away. And Jonesy disappeared into the alley that led to the steps up Telegraph Hill.

Jack finished her drink. A black sedan pulled up at the curb. Sergeant Dan Reynolds, a ruddy plainclothes vice cop in his early forties, lumbered out of the car. He tipped his hat back on his head and put his hands on his hips. "You okay, sir?" he asked Bill, who was sitting up again.

"I certainly ain't. That—freak—made a pass at my Sue Ann." He glared at Jack, who leaned against the wall, her arms crossed.

Reynolds shook his head. "Jack, Jack, Jack. Now, why would you want to do that?"

"I didn't."

Bill sputtered. "Bet'cher ass she did. Then she hauled off and *slugged* me."

Reynolds looked at Jack.

"He swung first," she said.

"Sure he did." Reynolds took a small notebook out of the pocket of his brown suit. "You want to press charges, sir?"

"Bet'cher ass I do. There oughta be a law against her kind."

"There is." Reynolds flipped the notebook open, licking the end of his pencil. "Name?"

"William Mast—" Bill hesitated. "Hey, listen. No one else gotta know about this, right?"

"You file charges, it's a matter of public record, sir." The pencil hovered over the paper. "The boys who cover the crime beat for the morning papers check every night."

"The *papers*?" Sue Ann's eyes went wide. "Bill, we don't—"

Bill stood up and dusted himself off. "I'm in insurance. Back home. If my good name got dragged through the mud with—" He let the worlds hang in the air and looked at his wife. "Maybe we oughta go back to the hotel?"

"You want to get a punch in first, sir?" Reynolds asked. "I'll hold on to her."

Jack barked a laugh. "The hell you will."

Bill raised both hands and clenched them into fists.

"Bill, you can't hit a *girl*!" Sue Ann cried.

He turned toward Jack, glaring as if he could shoot bullets out of his eyes, then let his hands drop. "You're right," he said with a sigh. "Let's go, Sue Ann."

"Suit yourself." Reynolds slipped the notebook back into his pocket. Jack stepped toward the door of the club.

"Not so fast." Reynolds turned, fast for a big guy, and pushed Jack up against the wall before she could move. He hip-checked her, pinning her, then groped her shirt front with both hands, squeezing, hard, a smile on his face. "Tied down again, huh? No brassiere, that's one."

Jack clenched her jaw and said nothing. They'd done this dance before, and it was no good hitting a cop. That could get you six months, and last time she'd gone to lockup she'd come out with a black eye and a couple of loose teeth. "Come on, Reynolds," she said in a voice as calm as she could manage. "I got another set to play."

"Don't think so. You've got men's shoes on and I'm in a betting mood tonight, going for the trifecta." He barred one arm across her chest and swiftly thrust his other hand into her trousers. He pulled up the edge of a wide elastic band. "Well, whad'ya know? BVDs. Too bad you got nothing to put in them—eh, *Jacqueline*."

"Bastard," Jack said. Her mouth was wet from the drinks and the word flew out in anger. A gobbet of spit landed on Reynolds's tie. "Oh, shit. That was just an—"

"An assault on an officer? Yes, it was." He let her briefs snap back and reached for his cuffs. "You just made my night, sweetheart."

He led her to the sedan, pushing her onto the cracked leather of the back seat, and got into the front. "O'Shea's on night shift. He's going to have *lots* of fun with you," he said through the grill. Siren off, he did a U-turn and drove off toward Portsmouth Square and the Hall of Justice.

Inside, the bartender flipped the lights back off. If there'd been more cops—a raid—she would have flashed them again, so Mona could open the back door to the alley. But not tonight. Tonight it was just Big Jack, drunk and unlucky again. She sighed. "Ah, Jack. You failed the three-garment test with a perfect zero, not a single piece of women's clothing on you."

A girl in a skirt and sweater reached for her beer and looked puzzled. "Huh?"

"The law says women can't dress like men. If the cops check, and you're wearing three bits of ladies' duds, you're in the clear."

Haskel ran a hand down her own clothes. Pants and a shirt, but their labels would distinguish them: women's slacks, a woman's blouse. And her pendant, if jewelry counted.

"It's easy enough to get around," another woman said.

Her hair was short and she wore a suit and tie, but pointed to her feet. "Black flats. That's one. And there's a little frill on my undies, top and bottom. No one sees *that* unless they're invited." She shook her head. "Jack's too proud."

"Jack was too drunk." The bartender squeezed a lime into a drink. "Reynolds wouldn't have come round if there hadn't been a fight."

"What fight?" A brunette in a cocktail dress asked. "I saw the lights flash."

"Jack and a tourist, Gloria."

"That's a shame. She was on fire tonight."

"Yep, she was." The bartender smiled at Haskel. "Another round?"

"No thanks. I'm going home." She lit a smoke as she headed out the door, then stopped, Viceroy in hand, when she saw Spike on the sidewalk, hands in her pockets, staring at her feet. Schoolgirl saddle shoes, Haskel noticed, her artist's eye filing away the detail. Everyone else had gone back inside.

"Reynolds got Jack," Spike said softly.

"I saw."

"She's in jail tonight. I don't know where I'm going to go."

"Why's that?"

"We share a flat, and I can't go home." Speaking, the deep honeyed voice was gone, replaced with that New

England drawl, now without a trace of arrogance or bravado.

"I don't follow. Jack won't be there."

"No, but sweet little Nancy will. Jack's new girlfriend. She earns her keep—how shall I put it?—entertaining gentlemen for cash. She'll be at it all night trying to make Jack's bail," Spike said with a sigh. "And Reynolds knows it. He'll be round with his goons about 3 a.m., and that's a party I'd rather miss."

"What will you do?"

"Sleep here, I guess. Mona's a good egg. She's used to waifs and strays, keeps a cot in back. I think it's left over from the Great War."

"Sounds uncomfortable."

"So I've heard. But it's either that or throw myself on the mercy of the mission, and I'm afraid I have no desire to be saved."

Haskel was quiet. She had a neat and ordered life and liked it that way. She hadn't thought much of this girl, at Franny's. But now she looked like a lost pup, and Haskel couldn't remember the last time anyone had moved her to tears. That song. That voice. She lit another cigarette off the glowing end of the first and came to a decision. "Do you snore?"

"Not that I've been told."

"I'm an early riser. I like to paint in the morning light."

"I can tiptoe like a lamb in slippers."

It was an odd negotiation. Neither said much, but each heard what she needed.

"I've got a studio in the Monkey Block, top floor. The couch folds out."

"Won't your husband mind?"

"He's at sea. I haven't seen him in a while." It had been almost four years, and Len had shipped out on a freighter one step ahead of the cops, but she didn't feel obliged to share those details.

"Oh." Spike looked startled. "Well, then. Sure." She glanced in at the clock over the bar. "Intermission's over. I'll find Bev, see if she can cover the piano for my last set." She turned down the alley to the stage door, then stopped. "Thanks."

"You're welcome." Haskel watched her go. What had she gotten herself into? Nothing. She was just a Good Samaritan. And that prickle at the back of her neck, the kind she hadn't felt in—ages? Just a chill from the ice in her drinks. That was all. She took one last drag on her cigarette, tossing it to the curb, and went back into Mona's.

"Bourbon. Rocks," she said to the bartender.

"I thought you'd gone home." She poured the jigger into a glass.

"I did, too. But I seem to have acquired a houseguest,

so I'll stay for another round." She put some coins on the counter. "You see, I only have the one key." She headed back for the second show.

SECRET CITY

SECRET CITY

Emily woke in a room with robin's-egg–blue walls, light streaming through a slanted glass ceiling. She yawned and stretched, turned over, and stared into the face of a hideous ebony fiend, its red tongue lolling from a mouth full of jagged, discolored teeth. Its crimson eyes bulged.

She gave a little shriek and sat bolt upright as her brain began to tick over, like an engine starting on a cold morning. Haskel's studio. The pull-out sofa. Bracing herself, she looked again. It was a monster, all right, but a painted one, lying propped on the drafting table a few feet from where she lay.

When her breathing slowed again, she called out, "Haskel?" No answer.

She slid out from under the blanket, stood, and immediately had to pee. The toilet was down the hall. All she wore was her white shirt and panties. Her trousers were bunched at the end of the bed, stiff formal serge that required buttoning and fastening and the untangling of suspenders. Not a pair she could simply slip on.

"Haskel?" Nothing. She padded barefoot into the other room, where there was a neatly made bed, a wardrobe, and a bureau. Hanging from a hook on the wall was a tartan bathrobe. She reached for it, stopped. The night before, after the couch had been unfolded, they had exchanged formal, awkward goodnights, in the way of strangers who've come together by circumstance more than choice, and each gone to sleep.

Borrowing a bathrobe felt like an unwarranted invasion of Haskel's privacy, a liberty Emily was in no way entitled to. Perhaps it was even the mysterious husband's robe, which would be a different, more unsettling intrusion. But her bladder was more insistent than her sense of etiquette, and she put the robe on, belting it loosely.

Emily was five-foot-eight, a tall girl. This robe's sleeves drooped over her wrists and the hem nearly brushed her ankles. She felt as if she were a child, playing dress-up in Daddy's wardrobe again.

She was, however, decent, and went down the hall to the lavatory, returning a few minutes later, much relieved. Still no sign of Haskel. Emily walked to the drafting table and stood over the painting, done not in oils or watercolors, as she expected, but in pastel chalks, a dozen of which lay in a wooden tray.

For all its gruesomeness, it was beautifully executed—the colors vivid, the composition balanced, drawing her eye to both the horrific face framed in an open window and the rough, pencil-sketched form of a girl in the bed below.

"You intrigue me, Haskel," she said aloud, as her stomach rumbled. Breakfast? She found a percolator, pushed the sleeves of the robe up to her elbows, and filled the coffeepot at the wide, stained sink. She set it on a hot plate, the metal housing spotted with bits of paint and what looked like glue. She was on the hunt for a can of coffee when the door to the hall opened.

"You're up," Haskel said. She had two paper sacks in the crook of one arm. "I see you've made yourself at home."

Emily looked down at the robe. "The toilet's down the hall, and I had a rather urgent—" She stopped, feeling herself blush with the effrontery of it. "I hope you don't mind."

"Not too much. It adds to your rescued waif-and-stray look." She held up one of the bags. "If you were trying to make coffee, you'll need this. I was out, and Graffeo's roasts theirs fresh every day." She set it down next to the carafe. "It's spoiled me for Maxwell House, I'm afraid."

"Smells heavenly," Emily said. She scooped the dark oil-slick grounds into the filter and turned on the hot plate. "What's in the white one?"

"Raspberry rings, from that little bakery on Columbus. I indulge myself whenever I sell a painting."

"You sold one this morning?"

"Well, not yet." Haskel smiled. "I don't entertain often, but even I know that a proper hostess needs to offer *something* in the way of breakfast."

"Even to waifs and strays?"

"Especially them." She ripped open the bakery bag and made it into a makeshift platter for the rings—two flat plaited wreaths of flaky pastry, as big as saucers, with ribbons of red jam woven through them like streamers on a maypole. Each confection glistened with icing sugar. "Sleep all right?"

"Much better than on Mona's army cot," Emily said. "Although I did have a bit of a fright, seeing *that* first thing."

"'The Gargoyle's Kiss.' Cover art for *Weird Menace*. Assuming I get it finished, you'll see it again on the newsstands in two months."

"Can't wait." Emily eyed a raspberry ring but heard her mother's voice—*now darling, it's the hostess who offers food*—and didn't reach for it. Her stomach rumbled again. She never ate much before a show, and yesterday afternoon's egg salad was a distant memory. She looked back at the painting. "You've got real talent, you know. Why do you paint such hideous things?"

"They pay the rent." Haskel cocked her head. "Why do you sing at Mona's—Spike?"

"Touché." She leaned against the edge of the table, rolling and tucking the sleeves of the robe, hoping they'd stay put. "I'm an odd duck, I suppose. Always have been. Unsuited for any respectable job."

"We have that in common. I wouldn't last ten minutes as a secretary." Haskel blew into two china mugs and, when nothing flew out, poured coffee into each.

"Nor I." She took the proffered mug. "Imagine doing that, day after day?"

"I can't. I've always worked on my own schedule, and dressed as I choose." She picked up one of the raspberry rings and nudged the paper in Emily's direction. "Breakfast is served."

There was nowhere to sit except the edge of the bed, and Emily didn't want to be the sort of guest who leaves crumbs in the sheets. She took the pastry and perched on a windowsill, one leg on the floor, the other bent in front of her.

"Is all your work for—?"

"The pulps? It is now. It's steady. I do covers for three different titles—and the new one you saw at Franny's—*Diabolical Dr. Wu Yang*. White slavery, Oriental fiends in opium dens, that sort of thing." She bit into her ring; a flaky shower of crumbs as delicate as snowflakes fluttered to the tabletop. "Don't know how long it will last, but ninety bucks a cover is nothing to sneeze at."

"Ninety!" Emily's leg dropped to the floor with a thump. "Ye gods and little fishes. Even sharing tips, I'm lucky to clear fifteen a week." She turned and stared at the monster with a look of awe and respect. "How fast do you work?"

"I can do two a month, if I get the assignments. There are a couple other artists vying for the same titles." She finished one last bite and reached for her cigarettes. "The fat months cover the lean. You know how that is."

"Do I ever. Before the fair opened again in May, Mona's was half empty. No tips, no groceries. Barely covered the rent. I'm trying to sock away as much as I can before the lean and hungry autumn."

"I thought you came from money."

"I did. Before I was thrown from the nest and cut out of the will."

"Black sheep?"

"Baaa," Emily mumbled through a mouthful of pastry.

"You trained to be a singer?"

"No, an English major. I thought I'd write for the *New Yorker* for a year, then produce a slim volume of jewel-like short stories." Emily put a dramatic hand to her forehead and saw Haskel barely suppress a laugh. "I know. One of those. Alas, ninety bucks does not fine literature pay."

"So how did you end up—?"

"Girls' school. Chapel and lots of jolly singing. Amateur theatricals, too. With my register, I got all the boys' parts. Turns out I can carry a tune."

"I'll say." Haskel ground out her smoke in an ashtray. "You were head and shoulders above the others last night."

"Aw, shucks, now." Emily felt herself starting to blush again, the ginger curse, and bent to examine a last bit of raspberry with the care a lepidopterist would give to a new species.

"Haskel!" a voice called from the hall door. "Open up. I have fish heads."

"Most buildings only have the milk delivered," Emily said.

"I don't have an icebox." Haskel put down her mug and headed for the door. "Besides, I take my coffee black."

Standing in the hall, holding a stained, newspaper-wrapped bundle dripping from one corner, was Helen Young. "Sorry," she said. "I tried to cover them, but they—" she stopped in midsentence when she saw Emily, barefoot and bathrobed, perched on the win-dowsill. "Well, well, well."

Both other women shook their heads. "It's not what you think," they said at the same time, then looked at each other.

"Jinx," Haskel said.

Emily laughed. "My brother Ned and I used to do

that." She felt a sudden ease as the shared joke lifted any awkwardness, like a breeze parting the fog, revealing an unexpected glimpse of the sunlit hills.

Helen put the sodden parcel in the sink. "It's not?"

"No. Reynolds hauled Big Jack in last night, and her sweetie, Nancy, was—entertaining—in my flat. Haskel let me stay here out of the goodness of her heart."

"And I am Marie of Romania," Helen said. "Scuttlebutt says Jack got ninety days."

"Hell's bells."

"Got that right. Do I smell coffee?"

"Help yourself." Haskel began to peel apart the newsprint and made a face. "Phew."

"I know. Not terribly fresh. That's why they aren't soup today. For your purposes, I didn't think it mattered." Helen looked around. "Do you have cream?"

"She takes hers black," Emily said in the serious tone of a newscaster.

"I see," Helen said in an amused, knowing voice. "Well, in that case, seeing as I have a delicate stomach—and a noon rehearsal—I'm off to Fong Fong's for a proper breakfast. You girls have fun." She winked. "With the fish, of course."

"Don't be cheeky," Haskel said. "Thanks."

"Alley raider, at your service." Helen put the empty mug down. "Abyssinia." She gave a two-finger salute and shut the studio door behind her.

"Well, there goes my good name." Emily wasn't entirely sure she was joking. Or that she cared. She pointed to the sink. "I do hope that's not our second course."

"Fish glue," Haskel said. She knelt down by the table and parted a striped curtain that concealed pots and pans, a carton of cleanser, a bottle of dish soap, and two cans of condensed soup. She set a big pot on the tabletop and began to toss in fish heads, bones, and skin. "Oh, good, she found some bladders after all." She held up a yellowish sac, smiling as if she'd gotten a tin of candies for Christmas, and threw it into the pot.

"Fish glue?"

"It's a fixative." She set the percolator on the table and filled the metal pot with water, fish heads bobbing on the surface, their filmy eyes staring up disconcertingly, then turned the hot plate's dial to Hi. The coils began to glow brighter. "You might want to open the window. It's not exactly potpourri."

Emily raised the frame half a foot. "What do you need to fix?"

"The painting."

"Is it broken?"

"No, just very delicate. The chalk. I like its texture, and it's essentially a powder, so the particles reflect light in a way that oil paint can't. Gives the color wonderful depth." She looked around for her cigarettes, lit one, and used it to gesture as she continued. "But that same—powderiness—means it's so fragile that one strong puff of air—imagine blowing out a birthday candle—can make a day's work just disappear."

"Poof."

"Poof. So I have to prepare the paper. Rough it up with a pumice stone and brush a coat of isinglass onto the back. It saturates the fibers, makes them more—receptive."

"What's isinglass?"

"Fish glue's society name."

"Why not use shellac? Or varnish?"

"They dull the colors, a sort of yellow haze, like cigar fug. This is a bit rank, but it's cheap and it works." She stirred the pot with a discolored wooden spoon. "It'll look like ancient cellophane, once the liquid's strained and it dries. Then I pulverize it with a mortar and pestle and add a bit of grain alcohol. Some goes in a jar, the rest in one of these." She reached under the sink again and held up a perfume atomizer.

"Eau de pêche?"

"Attracts alley cats by the score," Haskel said. "The mist settles without disturbing the surface. Two applications and the painting arrives at the publisher's intact." She looked into the pot, which had begun to bubble.

"This is enough for half a dozen covers."

"How on earth did you figure all that out?"

"Franny found some ancient recipe in one of her art books. She's—you're the English major—what's the crossword answer for someone who learns a little about everything?"

"Hmm. Know-it-all?"

Haskel chuckled. "That sounds more like you."

"Guilty as charged." She thought for a moment. "Polymath."

"That's it. Franny's a polymath. Among other things." Haskel turned the hot plate down. "These need to simmer for a few hours."

"I should go and let you work." Emily slid off the windowsill and bent to gather her clothes. "I'll turn this back into a sofa for you."

"Hang on a sec." Haskel looked at the half-finished painting, then back at the rumpled blanket. "I hadn't noticed, when it was a couch, but it's got just the right light from the window—" She tapped a finger to her lip. "You said that gave you a fright when you woke up?"

"I squealed like a girl."

"Could you do it again?"

"What?"

"Crawl under the covers, try a few poses for me?"

"I guess. I owe you for breakfast." She undid the robe's

sash, letting it slip off and puddle on top of her pants and jacket, then sat at the head of the bed and pulled the blanket up around her, holding it across her chest. "Like this?"

"Too awake." Haskel picked up a pencil and sketch pad. "Try this. It's the middle of the night. You're sound asleep, woken by a sound at the window. You turn and see—well, just what you saw. The gargoyle."

"Take two." Emily scooched down and turned toward the drafting table, raising herself on one elbow and widening her eyes with as much horror as she could muster in broad daylight.

"Good. Hold that." Haskel filled the page with swift, deft strokes, and turned to a fresh one. "Now sit halfway up, like you're in the middle of a startle."

"I thought you had dirty magazines for this sort of thing."

"They're *art* magazines, and I do, but the poses are never *quite* what I need. It's easier if I have a model." She swept the pencil across the page, frowned, turned to another and sketched in rapid, sweeping lines, brow furrowed, concentration complete.

Emily watched, initially fascinated by this glimpse into a real artist's process, and then less so as it grew repetitious. Not a spectator sport. "My arm's numb," she said after another minute.

"Sorry. Just one more, and I'll free you from artistic servitude." Haskel flipped to a clean page. "Lie on your side. Rumple the covers a bit."

"Yes, Mrs. DeMille," Emily mock grumbled, although she was finding the playacting rather a lark. It reminded her of midnight games in the dorm, of Jilly, of— She winced, not at the memory, but at all that had come after, and covered it by resettling herself, tugging at her shirt. It had rucked up in the middle of her back, a twisted, uncomfortable lump. She pulled one arm out of a sleeve, then the other, and let it drop to the floor. "Like this?"

"Not quite. A little more—" Haskel set the sketch pad down and knelt by the bed. "—like this." With one hand, she turned Emily's head slightly to the side, her fingers entwined, for a moment, in auburn curls. Emily felt her arms go all goosebumps. Their faces were inches apart. She could feel the warmth of Haskel's breath on her cheek, smell coffee and a drift of smoke.

A moment passed. Neither of them moved. Then she heard Haskel sigh and felt a tickle of hair against her neck, lips brushing her own, lightly at first, and then, when she offered no resistance—none at all—with unmistakable desire.

"Golly," Emily said, when there was air again.

"Shh." Haskel took off her own shirt and settled onto the bed, pushing the blankets down and away. Cupping a gentle hand on either side of Emily's face, she kissed her again, lips full and soft and tasting of raspberries. The springs creaked as they shifted, arms and legs twining until they were snugged together like pieces of a jigsaw puzzle, once jumbled and separate, but destined to fit exactly so.

• • •

Later, after, they lay with eyes half-closed against the midday sun. Emily's head nestled in the angle of Haskel's shoulder. Her thoughts tumbled, muddled, dulled with languor, tinged forever with the smell of *eau de pêche*, an odd but not unpleasant backdrop for the whole, surprising morning. Contentment and wonder, twined with translucent threads of melancholy that had so little to do with the woman in her arms.

She ran her fingers across a bare shoulder, trailing them down the chain of Haskel's necklace to her lightly freckled back, then paused. "What's that?" she asked, touching a shiny, flattened dimple the size of a pea. "And those," discovering others.

Haskel flinched, but did not pull away. She lay silent, and Emily's fingers stilled, unsure. Should she apologize? Say nothing? Pretend that—?

"Cigarette burns. Because I was a naughty girl."

"Your father *burned* you?"

"My mother. Dear old Ma." She took Emily's hand and kissed the knuckles, then sat up against the back of the couch and reached for her cigarettes.

"That's terrible."

"Yes." She drew her legs up, one arm around her knees. "I've never cared much for rules. Hers kept changing. What was conversation one day was somehow sass the next." She blew a smoke ring out into the air. "She's an angry, bitter woman. I learned to keep still. Drawing in the root cellar, in the garden shed, anywhere I was invisible."

"She found you."

"She hunted me."

Emily leaned against Haskel's shoulder again. "Is that why you paint monsters?"

"The monsters are easy. They come straight out of the stories I'm sent; they're the writers' nightmares, not mine. Although the good ones—" she shuddered. "I *have* slept with the lamp on a few times."

"And the victims?"

"Always girls. Writers seem to think we're interchangeable." A small, mirthless chuckle. "I leave the faces for last. I have to have a drink or two first." She got out of bed, paced to a shelf, picked out a magazine. A hunchback in a white lab coat leered at a girl covered only by a tendril of smoke, straining against thick leather straps that bound her to a gleaming table. Her hands were clenched, her mouth open in a silent scream.

"I know how that feels. Holding my breath. Making no sound. Sweating, heart racing, guts liquid—waiting for her to find me, *knowing* she was coming." She tapped the ghastly cover. "But look at that girl. She hasn't given up. The men who buy this won't see it, but I know. Because *I* got away." Haskel's jaw was set, her eyes fierce and bright. "*That* fear is on the paper now, not eating away inside me. Bit by bit, scream by scream. Like emptying a bucket with a teaspoon."

"How many paintings have you done?

"The first one of *these* was when I was still in art school. Spring of '33. So seven years, one or two a month." She counted, moving her fingers. "Close to a hundred by now."

"Is the bucket empty?"

"It's lighter."

Haskel put the magazine down and stepped to the window, crossing her arms over her full breasts, the pendant between them flashing with the movement. She was a handsome, muscular woman, not an ounce of extra flesh. Emily watched as Haskel bit her lip, realizing how much she'd revealed. The silence in the room grew awkward again. Emily lay in the tangle of bedclothes, then pulled her knees to her chest and rolled, an athletic move that left her standing in her own birthday suit, on the far side of the bed.

Haskel turned. "Are you leaving?"

"Do you want me to?"

"I don't know."

"Would you like a song first?"

"*What?*"

"Well, I thought, as long as we're sharing."

Haskel smiled, just a fraction. "Alright. Surprise me."

"I like 'The Way You Look Tonight.'" Emily's knees felt rubbery. She put one hand on the bookcase for support. "And this afternoon." She took a very deep breath to get the jitters out, and began to sing.

"Some day, when I'm awfully low, and the world is—" Her voice was smooth and deep and brave even as her hands shook. She had sung in the shower, and to countless audiences of strangers, but always with a costume or Spike's cocky, hip-shot artifice. This was different.

When she finished, Haskel sat on the bed, her eyes bright but no longer fierce. "Jesus," she said, part oath, part benediction. She leaned back and held out her arms. "No. I don't think I want you to leave."

• • •

The light was golden before they got out of bed again,

laughing when Emily's stomach grumbled loud enough to startle them both out of a languid drowse. They dressed, Haskel in clean slacks and shirt, Emily in Spike's outfit.

"I'll need food and some other clothes. In that order," Emily said, watching Haskel strain the fish heads and pour the gelatinous result into an enameled pan.

"Where's your flat?"

"Three blocks up from Mona's."

"There's a deli on the way. We'll have a picnic supper." Haskel wrapped the remains of the fish in yesterday's *Chronicle* and washed her hands. "This will make us friends with their tom."

They got thick sandwiches of salami and smoked ham and salty cheese on crusty bread, with some sweet peppers and onions. A jug of homemade wine was only thirty-five cents, so they splurged. Haskel carried the bag of food, Emily swung the bottle by its neck as they walked up Montgomery, a street of cafés and low brick offices that rose steeply when it crossed Broadway. Now bow-windowed buildings and weathered frame houses clung to the precarious sides of Telegraph Hill like goats. From an open window came the sound of someone expertly practicing a trumpet.

"This is me," Emily said when they reached Green Street. "Grey one." The front porch sagged; by the doorbell were four gummed labels. "They sliced it into apartments in the '20s," Emily said. "No charm, but it's cheap—five bucks a week—and it came furnished."

"Horrible green or florals?"

"The sofa is both." She gestured to a window. "My room must have been a pantry. Lots of shelves, not enough room to swing a cat."

"Look." Haskel turned toward the wall of a building across the street. The beige stucco was dappled with shadows and lit with butter-colored western light. "I love this time of day. Feels like anything is possible."

Emily nodded. "It reminds me of the illustrations in a book I had as a girl—*The Arabian Nights*."

"Maxfield Parrish?"

"Yes. Everything seemed magic."

"Magic light is the best kind for a picnic, don't you think?" Haskel started up the hill. "Come on. We'll sit on the Greenwich Steps, come back for your worldly goods."

"They're not much. I left school rather abruptly."

"Why?"

"My—friend—and I were caught one morning. The alarm hadn't gone off."

"They booted you for missing a class?"

"No, for being in Jilly's bed." She shifted the wine to her other arm. "I had enough money for a train ticket, so I came here. It's where all the black sheep end up.

New York was closer, but proximity to my family was, well—less than desirable. Besides, I'd had my fill of snow."

"Me too." Haskel linked her arm through Emily's. Now the sidewalk was so steep that shallow steps were cut into the concrete. To their left, houses climbed in vertical tiers on winding streets and tiny lanes only half a block long. On the right, sheer rocky cliffs spilled down to the waterfront, two hundred feet below.

Greenwich Street, a paved thoroughfare for most of its length, became rickety-looking wooden steps that zigzagged down the sandstone face, passing under some stilt-raised houses. It flanked tiny nineteenth-century cottages, wound through gardens and grottoes and stretches of brush-dotted bare stone that looked more like a canyon from the Wild West than a modern, cosmopolitan city.

Partway down was a landing, the boards laid horizontally across a large granite outcropping. "This is perfect," Haskel said. She swung herself down to the weathered planks and dangled her legs over the precipice.

Emily sat next to her, settling the jug of wine with a muffled thump. "Jeepers."

"You haven't been up here before?" Haskel pulled the cork out with her teeth and took a swig.

"Didn't know it existed."

"San Francisco is full of secrets." She unwrapped one of the sandwiches and handed it across.

"I'll say." Emily felt as if she had ventured much farther than a ten-minute walk. Below them were the flat-roofed meatpacking plants and warehouses that lined the waterfront, the wharves sticking into the bay like splayed fingers. The smell of salt water and mud, diesel fuel and roasting coffee wafted up to their perch, high above the world. Whistles and bells sounded from the busy port, shutting down for the evening. Off to the left, out of sight, a foghorn echoed.

The hill behind them blocked the sun. What had been a golden summer evening was transforming, moment by moment, into a world of shadows, a thousand shades of gray punctuated by the white globes of streetlights, a few piercing streaks of neon. The lights of the city winked on around them, reflecting out onto the water, a flat, dark void with the man-made paradise of Treasure Island in its center.

San Francisco was a beautiful city, but it was a city—brick and stone, grays and browns, vertical lines, right angles, and uniform patterns of windows repeated building by building, block by block, rectangular and regular.

Directly in front of them, two miles out, they watched as another city, made of lath and plaster, changed into its evening clothes. By day, it was a transient chimera of palaces and minarets, curving courts, and colonnaded temples. Now, bursting through the dusk, searchlights fanned out toward the stars like the hand of God, and ten thousand colored floodlights turned the stucco castles into glowing, glittering jewels.

Emily gasped. "Does that happen every night?"

"Every time I've come to watch." Haskel passed the bottle. "You've seen the fair, right?"

"Not like this. I feel like I'm Dorothy, and that must be Oz." She stared, her mouth open. "Only it's not just the Emerald City—it's sapphire and ruby and—"

Haskel laughed and put an arm around Emily, pulling her close. "Let's go there, you and I. Let's take a journey to the Magic City and have drinks beside a sparkling fountain."

"Tonight?"

"No, you have to sing, and I have a painting to finish. Next—" She thought for a moment. "Next Wednesday. We'll take my cover downtown to Railway Express and catch the ferry, make a day of it."

Emily looked out at the island, a block of color afloat in a featureless sea. "I'd like that. Wednesday's a slow night."

"So it's a date." Haskel leaned over and kissed her, their lips tingling from wine and peppers.

"Funny, isn't it?" Emily said a few minutes later.

"What?"

"We've done this wrong way round. A first date *after* we—well, you know." She felt suddenly shy, not wanting to name their day, to make it vulgar, or coy and coded. At a loss for words. That was unsettling. Words were her refuge.

"I told you I've never cared much for rules."

"I'm glad."

"So am I." Haskel kissed her again, on the cheek this time. She stood and stretched. "If you want to rescue anything from your flat before work, we should get moving."

Emily got to her feet and leaned on the railing, gazing out at the fairyland across the water, then turned to link her arm in Haskel's. They retraced their steps through the patches of yellow lamplight from the houses that lined the moon-shadowed stairs.

THE MAGIC CITY

Haskel finished the gargoyle painting late Monday night and misted it with *eau de pêche* before she and Emily went to bed, giving it a second spraying the next afternoon.

She was surprised how easy it was to make room for Emily—in the studio, in her life. That had unfolded as naturally as a newly hatched moth; now she couldn't imagine the space without her.

When they'd returned to the flat on Green Street, they found it a shambles—overflowing ashtrays, greasy cardboard containers of chow mein, clothes strewn about—with men on the stairs and in the small kitchenette, drinking and waiting their turn with sweet Nancy.

Emily packed her things and scrawled her notice, leaving a week's rent; wolf whistles and ungentlemanly offers followed them down the dingy hall and out onto the street.

"I can store my suitcase backstage," Emily said, a block down Montgomery Street. "Not my typewriter, though. I'd hate to lose that." She spoke bravely, but her mouth was pinched and her grip on the case was white-knuckled.

"We'll take it all to my place."

"Are you sure?"

"Absolutely." It was the right thing to say; Haskel had not been sure at all. It was one thing to spend an afternoon in bed with a beautiful woman, and quite another to set up housekeeping the same day. She'd been on her own for more than five years, and it had suited her. But Emily's pinched look had vanished, replaced by her now-endearing impish grin.

Haskel rose early. She made coffee and painted until midmorning. Emily padded in to kiss the back of her neck and admire her progress. She curled up on the couch, writing in a leather-bound journal with a blue marbled fountain pen or reading with the intensity of a schoolgirl cramming for exams, working her way through the pulps on Haskel's shelf, pausing now and then to comment.

"*Your* madman was much better than the one in the story."

"*Why* would she go down the stairs with an evil scientist in the first place?"

"Most of these are *awful*."

"No one buys them as literature," Haskel said without turning around.

They had a light supper each night before Emily dressed and walked over to Mona's. Haskel stayed in.

She put on a record—symphonies, not singers—and sketched, trying to keep herself from thinking about all the women salivating over "Spike."

She was not a possessive person, thought of herself as a free thinker. This was different. Fragile and new and more precious than she would have imagined. That both warmed and unsettled her.

Early Wednesday, Haskel pinned the corners of the heavy art paper to a sheet of corrugated cardboard and set it into a shallow wooden crate, then screwed down the lid. Early on, she had used tacks, but the vibrations from the hammer blows had ruined the edge of one painting where the fixative had not quite settled.

She stenciled GLASS FRAGILE GLASS in red paint, the only way to insure the box was handled with even a minimum of care. She changed into a plaid Viyella shirt and wool slacks. "You ready?" she called.

"Almost." Emily buttoned a yellow silk blouse over a pair of brown trousers, a sweater draped over one shoulder. Haskel had noticed that although her clothes were few, they had once been expensive, high-end labels that now showed signs of having been worn and laundered many times over. "I have sunglasses, sturdy shoes, and last year's guidebook."

"That ought to do it."

They left the painting for shipment at the Railway Express office on Folsom Street. Unencumbered, they strolled east to the Ferry Building, whose tower anchored the end of Market Street.

The line for tickets was long. They paid their dimes and boarded the ferry, crowded on all sides by men in suits and hats, women in daytime dresses, a few with furs draped around their shoulders. They made their way to the railing of the upper deck just as the steam whistle sounded, loud and shrill, and the three-hundred-foot boat moved out into the open waters of the bay.

"I never get tired of the view from here," Haskel said as the city receded, its stone towers square and solid against blue sky. "I see patterns—lines of streets and contours in the hills—that aren't visible when I'm walking." She curled an arm around Emily's shoulder, realized what she was doing, and pulled away, looking around. No one had noticed, and there were other girls whose hands or arms were linked in friendship, so she slipped hers into the crook of Emily's elbow, and felt a reassuring squeeze in return.

They stared back at the city until the babble of voices around them changed and, like a tennis match, everyone's head swiveled to look the other way. Treasure Island loomed two hundred yards ahead, close enough to see the carvings on the art-deco towers and pastel walls, gleaming and beckoning in the noonday sun, as if this routine ferry crossing had taken them to another world in the time it took to drink a cup of coffee.

The crowd rushed to disembark, jostling and pushing toward the wonders that awaited. Haskel was glad she was so tall; she could see over most of the hats, and guided Emily through seams in the fabric of humanity until they could pay the fifty-cent admission and were allowed to enter the walled city. They stopped in the lee of a building, and Emily unfolded the map from her guidebook.

"I want to go to the Fine Arts Palace and look in on a friend," Haskel said. "But that's all the way over in the far corner, half a mile's walk." She pointed. "If we went *here* first, we could cut through the—"

"Haskel?" a voice called, interrupting her proposed itinerary.

She turned. It was Franny, dressed in her usual tunic and slacks, a pair of round celluloid sunglasses obscuring her eyes. With her was an unfamiliar young girl in a sprigged cotton dress, the strap of a battered leather satchel slung across her chest like a crossing guard.

"Franny!" Haskel gave the older woman a hug. "What are the odds? Must be fifty thousand people here today."

"Kismet," she replied. "We were destined to meet in this unusual—" She stopped abruptly when she noticed Emily behind the flapping map. Franny smiled.

"Well. I see my nefarious plan worked."

"What plan?"

"I thought the two of you would hit it off. Hello, Emily."

"Hullo, Franny. Who's *your* friend?"

"Ah—where are my manners? Ladies, may I present Miss Polly Wardlow, late of London." She put an arm around the girl; Polly was half a head taller. She had pale blue eyes and wore her brown hair in two stubby braids. "Polly, these are my friends Emily Netterfield and Loretta Haskel."

"Just Haskel is fine."

Polly shook hands all around.

"Are you here on vacation?" Emily asked.

"No," Polly said. "I'm a sort of war refugee. With France fallen, my father didn't think England safe for me on my own. The army needed his expertise and he's overseas somewhere."

"What's he do?"

"He's a magician." She smiled at their startled looks. "It's not as far-fetched as it might seem. Magicians deal in deception and illusion, and camouflage of a sort. Useful against the enemy. I'm only guessing, of course. It's all very hush-hush."

Haskel felt a bit ashamed that she'd forgotten a lot of the world was actually at war. It seemed so unlikely on a clear summer day, here in the midst of cloud-cuckoo-land.

"We're distant relatives, on her mother's side. Great-aunts or some such," Franny said. "She'll stay with us until she starts Stanford in the fall."

"Stanford? How old are you?"

"Sixteen."

"That's impressive."

"Is it? I'd hoped to go to Oxford, but the war—" She faltered. "I queried Harvard and Yale, but did you know *neither* of them accepts women?"

"I'd heard." Emily laughed. "My father's a dean at Yale—classics." She looked around and turned to Franny. "Where's Babs?"

"Off entertaining her sister and her niece at the carnival rides. The child turned seven a few weeks ago, and this is her birthday treat. We're meeting up with them for drinks and a bite at five. Why don't you join us?"

Haskel and Emily exchanged glances. "Thanks," said Haskel. "Where are you headed now?"

"The science exhibits," Polly said. "I'm going to study chemistry and physics at university, and I want to see your newest technology."

"Not following in your father's footsteps," Haskel observed.

"Performing, no. Although I do enjoy his workroom.

That's where Father says the real magic happens."

"Science is on our way to the arts." Emily refolded the map. "We'll walk through with you."

One of the least decorative structures at the fair, the Hall of Science was an **L**-shaped building where several dozen exhibits demonstrated the latest in tooth powders, disinfectants, and tuberculosis prevention, none of which interested them. At the atom-smashing cyclotron, Polly pulled a small notebook and a mechanical pencil from her satchel and began taking copious notes.

"That's what Babs's sister Terry does," Franny said.

"Smashes atoms?"

"More or less. She's a nuclear chemist—think Madame Curie. Radium, radiation, energy from atoms, that sort of thing."

"Those pesky glowing rocks," Emily said wryly.

"Indeed."

Haskel whistled. "And Babs does that high-level math? Wonder what it was like, growing up with those two?"

"Challenging, I'd imagine," Franny replied.

The adjoining building, the Palace of Electricity, was much more entertaining. They stood in a huge crowd to listen to Pedro the Vodor, a machine that could "talk" when its pert young operator pressed a sequence of keys and pedals.

"*Patience is nec-ess-ary,*" it said in a modulated

monotone. "*So is ex-peer-ee-ence.*"

Further on, Polly sputtered at the marquee of the General Electric pavilion—HOUSE OF MAGIC. "It's *science*, not bloody magic."

"Maybe they thought it would sound—friendlier—to Mr. and Mrs. America," Emily said. "Your average Joe doesn't understand science. Makes him feel stupid."

"Bollocks," Polly said with a snort. "Science is how we understand the world. It doesn't need to be difficult. Making it mystical and hocus-pocus just muddies the waters."

"Franny. You *must* invite her to your next dinner party," Haskel said.

They gave short shrift to the newest marvels in vacuum cleaners, sewing machines, typewriters, and mimeographs but gaped when they saw Westinghouse's seven-foot robot—Willie Vocalite. He moved, nodded his head, and smoked cigarettes. None of them was sure how that would be useful.

"Have you done covers for any science-fiction titles?" Emily asked Haskel.

"No. I tried, but I can't draw ray guns or rockets to save my skin. They all looked like they were made from kitchen appliances. Not very thrilling."

The group parted ways at the exit. "It's almost one now," Franny said. "Meet us in the Gayway at Threlkeld's?"

"Scones," Polly said with a dreamy smile. She pronounced the word as if it rhymed with *bronze*.

"A crumbly English biscuit," Franny explained. "I promised her a little taste of home. Two weeks of travel forced her to consume all *manner* of barbaric American food." She winked at Polly.

"I did take a fancy to your tomato pie."

"Lupo's," Emily and Haskel said together. Then, "Jinx," in one voice. Haskel wanted to kiss her, right there in front of everyone, but—

"And with that, we're off to view the arts," she said instead. "See you at five."

"Give my best to Diego," Franny called after them.

"Will do." Haskel waved over her shoulder as she and Emily walked toward the Tower of the Sun. The whole fair was on a grand scale, an imaginary ancient civilization, a Biblical epic come to life: the Court of Reflections, the Arch of Triumph, the Court of Flowers.

The fine arts building was round-roofed and lowslung. They paid the twenty-five-cent admission and found the cavernous space marked ART IN ACTION. The floor was divided by partitions and low walls into a series of ateliers—lithographers, weavers, ceramicists. At each tiny studio, people gaped at real artists at work.

"Beats staring at old masters," Emily said as a muscular man pulled a print off a flat, inked stone. "It's like watching you paint."

"You owe me a few quarters, then." She pointed to the far wall, where scaffolding extended from floor to ceiling, partially concealing a vast mural in bright, intense colors. "We're headed over there."

"Wait. You mean to tell me that the Diego you're going to say 'hi' to is Diego *Rivera*?" Emily's mouth dropped open. "He's famous. He was in *LIFE* magazine. You *know* him?"

"He was painting the mural at the Art Institute when I was a student. He'd invite a few of us over to his place, after classes. That opened the door to another world for me. Art and culture, a way of life I'd never imagined—with a side of debauchery." She gave a rueful smile.

The upper portions of the wall were finished, bright with colors, alive with figures that wove around each other like a tapestry. The bottom three feet had penciled shapes incised into still-white plaster. Haskel pointed to a rotund giant with unruly black hair, standing on a platform halfway up. He wore paint-spattered dungarees and a chambray work shirt, the sleeves rolled up over dark arms.

"Diego!" Haskel called.

Heads turned to see who was so casual with the master. But the man continued painting with small, precise strokes of blue. When he finished, he set the brush down, wiped his hands, and finally turned.

Haskel held up a hand. "Diego!"

He spotted her and smiled. "Lorita! *Uno momento.*" He gestured to an assistant, pointed to the area he'd painted, and tapped on the man's watch. The man nodded twice, and Diego Rivera, rather nimbly for a man of his bulk, climbed down one of the ladders that descended to the floor.

"Lorita." He took both her hands in his own. He was only a bit taller than Haskel, but would have made two of her in girth. "What a nice surprise." He kissed her once on each cheek. "And you have brought me another beauty?" he said. His protruding eyes twinkled behind round gold-framed glasses, like an avuncular bullfrog.

"Diego Rivera, my friend Emily Netterfield."

He bowed and kissed Emily's hand. "Lorita still has a fine eye for women, I see. You are also a painter?"

"No, I sing."

"In the city? Where? I will come and bring my friends and they will buy many drinks."

"You probably don't know it—Mona's Club 440?"

"Mona's! Of course. I have not been there myself, but others speak of it. When my—" he paused, "—my Frida, when she arrives next month, I will take her. She can wear her suit, and that she will enjoy."

"How is she?" Haskel asked.

"Not well," he said with a frown. "She is never well, but this year—*madre de dios*! Her kidneys, her spine again. She takes many drugs and drinks too much. I worry, but—" He held up his hands. "I divorced her last year. Did you know?"

"No. What—?" Haskel stopped herself. With the two of them, it could be anything: his mistresses, her affairs—with men *and* women—his temper, *her* outbursts.

"It was a mistake," he said sadly. "She is lost without me. When she is here, we will reconcile, I think." He mopped his brow with a crumpled handkerchief. "But what of you, Lorita? You are still with—?"

"Len? Only legally."

"Ah. But you are happy? You are working?"

"Both." She lit a cigarette, offered him one. He accepted and indicated that they should step away from the open cans of varnish and turpentine.

"Still painting for those horrid stories?" When she nodded, he shook his head. "Such talent, this one. Does she make *art*? No. She entertains teenage boys with their hands down their trousers."

"It's a living, Diego."

"So is this." He swept his arm around to the mural. It was more than twenty feet tall and ran the full width of the building, at least seventy-five feet. "*Unión de la Expresión Artística del Norte y Sur de este Continente. The* critics call it 'Pan American Unity.' *Que chingados?*" He looked around, found an empty tin, and dropped his cigarette into it with a quick hiss. "At least this one, they let me finish it, eh? Not like that *pinche idiota,* Rockefeller. *Cabrón.*"

"What happens to it after the fair closes?" Haskel asked.

"I will continue, without the tourists watching, and then it will go to a college library."

Emily stared at the huge fresco. "You're going to *move* it?"

"It is five panels, hung on steel frames. They are each quite large, but from the beginning, we had planned this." He shrugged. "Engineers with cranes and trucks. It is not my job."

"Señor!" his assistant called from above.

Rivera waved. "I must get back to work, before the plaster dries. The colors must penetrate, become *part* of the wall." He smiled. "Frida has some work in the gallery. Go and see it. Her health grows worse, but her vision—" He kissed his fingertips with a loud smack. "She is like an angel forced to paint purgatory. Not unlike yourself, eh?" He patted Haskel's cheek. "*Adiós, hasta luego.*" He climbed the ladder back to the platform.

"You didn't tell me you knew *famous* people," Emily said as they entered a smaller corridor.

"You never asked."

The crowds were more sparse in the galleries. Tourists flocked to the fair for pageants and parades and thrills, not for contemplation. In a few minutes, they stood before Frida Kahlo's *Self-Portrait,* nearly a private viewing.

Emily stared. "That's—intense."

"She is. When I knew her she was 'just' Diego's wife. She'd exhibited one or two paintings. The headline in the papers was 'Wife of the Master Mural Painter Gleefully Dabbles in Works of Art.'" Haskel snorted. "Dabbles. She was furious, and let me tell you, *that's* something to see."

Emily took a step back. "I'm not sure I'd want her watching from my parlor wall."

The background was a vivid chartreuse, the woman pictured severe, unsmiling, her eyes staring out at them under a single line of heavy dark brow. Her black hair was wound with purple yarn and covered with a netting. She wore a simple white dress and a necklace made of bone and shell. A faint mustache shadowed her upper lip.

"I have a mustache," Emily said.

Haskel laughed. "No you don't."

"I mean, I own one. Theatricals."

"Frida's is real. It tickles."

"How do you know?"

Haskel leaned against the wall and lit a cigarette. "One

night, Frida and Diego threw a party. Artists and communists, lots of beards. The apartment was so packed it was hard to breathe. Frida and I ended up in a corner of the back porch, drinking this raw Mexican whiskey with a worm in the bottle. Potent stuff. She talked and I listened. You think *I* paint monsters—" She blew out a stream of smoke. "She's the one who taught me. Frida's been in pain—terrible, unthinkable pain—most of her life. Her art is the only way she gets through it. We talked until four in the morning—about taking the pain, the rage—the terror—getting it onto the canvas, *daring* the viewer to accept it. We drained the bottle, ate the worm, and ended up in their bed."

"You *slept* with her?"

"Only once. She was passionate—my god—but a bit much for me. I was *very* young."

Emily said nothing. She turned away, her arms tight across her body.

"You look upset."

"I have to pee." She laughed. "Did you think you'd shocked me with your wicked past, that I'd drop you like a hot potato?"

"It did occur to me."

"Well, not this afternoon." She looked around. "Let's go somewhere with a restroom and some food. I'm hungry."

"You're always hungry."

"You survive on coffee and cigarettes."

"Only when I'm working." Haskel thought for a minute. Most of the restaurants were over by the Gayway, on the other side of the island. In between there was only the Food and Beverage Building, with free samples of Junket custard, baked beans, or orange drink. Where—? She snapped her fingers. "The Yerba Buena Club."

"It's members only."

"It is." She tapped her pocket. "Babs joined back in '38, because of her job at the university, and she sponsored me. It was ten bucks, but she said it would come in handy—it's the only bar on this side of the fair."

"Lay on, MacDuff. I'm thirsty and nature is calling."

The building was streamlined and modern, all vertical lines and glass, abutting the port where the Pan Am Clippers landed. Inside it was elegant, with atrium gardens, a dining room, even a beauty shop.

"I'm sorry, this is a private club," a woman in a dark, severe suit said as they walked in. She did not sound sorry at all.

"Yes," Haskel replied. "I'm a member." She held out the card, which the woman examined with more scrutiny than was necessary, handing it back with a tight, polite smile. "No slacks in the dining room," she said. "You may use the lounge."

Many heads swiveled to see who had arrived. To a

woman, the others were in day dresses or suits with smart hats and smug looks, glaring scandalized at the newcomers' pants and bare heads. The hostess, with another tight smile, showed them to a table in a corner that overlooked an extravagant garden.

Emily whispered, "We're not their kind of women, are we?"

"I hope we never are." She gave Emily's knee a squeeze under the table.

They ordered club sandwiches and beers. When Emily returned from the restroom, she reported it was so fancy that each towel had its own attendant. Haskel burst out laughing, provoking another round of withering glances from the *ladies* of the club.

"My mother would fit right in," Emily said. "I bet everyone here is a Republican, and they're all voting for Wilkie. I don't see why. It's Roosevelt who has all the *ex-peer-ee-ence*."

This time Haskel laughed so hard she almost snorted beer out her nose. She couldn't remember the last time she'd felt so relaxed, when everything felt like a private joke the rest of the world couldn't share. As if she'd known Emily for years, as if they'd grown up together. It felt so easy. Nothing to prove, nothing to pretend.

They made up names for the hatted women: Winifred and Cordelia and Ursula, who wore a fashionable snood.

"In the society pages, she would be Mrs. DeWitt Ludlow Fitzbottom," Emily said.

"Of the *Burlingame* Fitzbottoms?"

"Of course, Millicent. Where did you think, Petaluma?"

"Now Florence, let's not be vulgar."

They left the club and ambled through the southeast corner of the fair. The wind was fierce, pressing their clothes to their bodies, snapping flags, keeping every tree and shrub in constant motion, a waving sea of color.

"I envy Franny and Babs," Emily said as a couple rode by them in a rickshaw, the man with his arm around the woman's shoulders.

"Why's that?"

"They make it look so easy, like they were an actual married couple." She frowned. "At Mona's, the regulars seem to think they have to *pick*—who's the boy, who's the girl. Babs and Franny aren't like that. They're just two women sharing a life together."

"I know. If I'm in pants, I must be butch. If I wear my hair down, or have lipstick on, I'm a femme."

"One customer told me that I *had* to choose, or I wasn't really—" Emily was quiet. They passed the Hall of the Western States. "Wonder what she'd make of you? You're married. For convenience?"

"No. I was in love with the guy, at first." Haskel stopped to light a cigarette, shielding the flame from the

---

wind with a cupped hand. "I'll confess, I have a checkered past. I've played for both teams."

"A Gillette blade."

"What?"

"Double-edged. Cuts both ways. But I don't get it. How—?"

"How I could ever eat garlic bread and hot fudge with the same mouth?"

"Yes." Emily laughed at the unexpected image.

"Like that. But until last week, it'd been a while since I did either." Haskel slipped her arm into Emily's. "So how do *you* fit into the grand scheme of things?"

"I'm not sure I do. I like trousers, but I don't see why being comfortable should be considered a *man's* privilege. Or smoking. Or drinking. By those lights, we're *all* men."

"I'm glad you're not."

"Me too. I mean, I was a tomboy, good at sports—that's where the name Spike came from, a wicked volleyball shot. I could keep up with the boys, but was never boy-crazy. You know. Then I met Jilly and—well—" She looked away, out at the whitecaps on the bay. "Schoolgirl crush, some said. Just a phase. T'wasn't. Obviously."

"I'm glad of that, too."

Now they could hear the barkers and calliopes, the

happy screams and din of the Gayway. They reached the illuminated pillars that marked its entrance a few minutes before five. That section of the fair had the chaotic air of cheap desperation. One last chance for fun, fun, fun, a sweeping boulevard of flash and neon, useless gimcracks, and thrill-seeking pleasures. The carnival smells of cotton candy, frying doughnuts, and motor oil mixed with the salt air and tang of seagull droppings.

"Who on earth named it the *Gay*way?" Haskel mused aloud.

"Some woman won a contest. Do you think the men in charge have any idea it's—?"

"No. They would have picked the runner-up."

They passed the Cyclone coaster, the Octopus, incubator babies, Ripley's Odditorium, the midget village, and "virgins in cellophane," aiming for a white tower with S-C-O-N-E-S spelled out vertically in huge red letters.

"You made it," Franny said. "Babs, look what I found."

Babs turned from the Threlkeld's counter. She handed Polly a waxed-paper-wrapped bundle, a bit of raspberry jam oozing from one side, and smiled at the new arrivals. "Well, well. She said you two were—"

"And we are," Emily said dryly. "Millicent, I think the neighbors approve."

"How very kind of them." Haskel squatted down. "You must be Suzie?"

"Suze," said the stocky blond child. "Like ooze." She had a blunt bowl haircut and a smear of mustard across one cheek. "I want to go *home* now."

"Hot dogs, ice cream, and pony rides aren't the best combination," a woman with honey-blond hair said. "I'm Terry Gordon, Babs's sister. I'm afraid we're on our way back to Berkeley. Long day, and *some*one's getting cranky." She held out her hand to the child. "Come on, sweetie. Let's go ride the boat. Nice to meet you," she said to the others. "I'll take a rain check for that drink."

"I'm *bushed*," Babs said. "Suze wanted to see *every*thing. I love her to pieces, but I'm ready for a tall cold one and some adult conversation."

Emily opened the guidebook. "The Estonian Village has a beer garden, and the Chinese Village has a cocktail lounge."

"We can have Chinese any time," Babs said. "Let's be adventurous and explore Estonian cuisine."

"What about Polly?"

Polly polished off the last of her scone and crumpled the paper. "What about me?"

"You have to be twenty-one to enter a drinking establishment," Franny told her.

"Oh. Well. Just a tick." She pulled a lipstick, compact, and comb from her satchel, applying the makeup quickly and expertly, then undid her braids, combed her hair, and fashioned it into an elegant French twist. "There," she said. "Do I pass muster?"

"You do. Wow."

"Stagecraft is all illusion."

The Estonian Village, three acres of quaint red-and-green buildings with high gables and turrets, was at the far west end of the Gayway. At the entrance to the beer garden, Polly handed the satchel to Haskel. "Here goes." She stepped up. "We require a table for five, my good man," she said with an arch look, her Britishness fully unfurled.

"Yes, ma'am. Right this way." He led them to a table.

"That worked," Haskel said when they were seated.

"We had a rather fierce headmistress at Giles Hall. She could simply *wither* with one glance. And Americans—even Estonians, it seems—are putty for a posh accent."

"You're full of tricks."

"You should see my exploding paint."

"Really?"

"Truly. I've created all sorts of whiz-bangs for Father's act."

"I thought you were going to be a scientist."

"There's loads of science behind good stage magic." She looked down at her menu. "What is 'chicken in the rough'?"

"A rare Estonian delicacy?" Franny guessed.

No, the waiter explained, it was fried chicken, shoe-string potatoes, and hot biscuits, to be eaten with the fingers. Napkins were provided, but no silverware.

"May I see the guidebook?" Polly asked once they'd placed their orders.

"Sure." Emily slid the thick paperbound book across the checkered oilcloth.

Polly leafed through the pages. "Oh. That sounds bloody marvelous."

"What does?" Emily leaned over.

"At night, they switch the lighting system to fluorescent tubes and ultraviolet radiation, which alters the perceived color composition in the various sectors."

"In English, please?" Haskel said, then laughed. "Sorry. In non-scientific terms?"

"The buildings turn different colors at night."

"Yes. It's really spectacular."

"It's the technique I'm keen to observe. It might be something Father could use to great effect." She read on. "Throughout the island, a concealed, indirect lighting system was installed, with beams in fantastic arrays shooting from mysterious places."

"Sounds like more science fiction," Emily said.

Haskel rolled her eyes. "It's definitely an *ex-peer-ee-ence.*" All of them laughed.

"Actually," the girl said, "seeing *any*thing brightly lit at night will be a delight for me. We've had blackout curfews for almost a year. No house lights, streetlights, no electric signs in Piccadilly or the West End. London feels like a ghost town after dark."

"Then we'll stay for the fireworks tonight," Babs declared. "They put on a magnificent show, every evening."

"Really? That would be splendid. And here I—" Polly bit her lip, wadding her napkin in embarrassment. "I'm afraid, on the train, I was rather dreading—"

"Ah." Franny chuckled. "You thought you were being banished to the maiden aunts, trapped for the rest of the summer in a dark, musty house with horsehair sofas and fussy doilies?"

"Along those lines." Polly sat back with a relaxed grin. "But you're all—well, you're all so jolly *fun*."

They finished their beers as shadows in the courtyard lengthened and the light faded on the walls around them. "Time for the show," Babs said. They left the Estonians and strolled toward the looming statue of Pacifica, crossing an avenue that gave a clear view of the western horizon and San Francisco, where city lights were winking on in their geometric order.

Emily tugged at Haskel's arm. "Look." She pointed across the water to the white cylinder of Coit Tower atop

Telegraph Hill. "You can see our steps, midway down the hill."

Our steps. Haskel felt an unexpected warmth. If one of them had been a man, she would have swept Emily into her arms. Sweethearts embracing at sunset, how charming, people would think. But they wouldn't, would they? They would turn away and mutter in disgust. She could only nod and attempt a smile.

They entered a court a thousand feet long that stretched from Pacifica to the Tower of the Sun, light standards as tall as buildings every twenty feet, hung with vertical blue-and-white striped banners. Suddenly—by magic or science or art or an amalgam of the three—the hidden lights came on, all at once. In a symphony of illumination, the world around them changed in an instant.

Windowless apricot walls became green and amber and pink against the deep blue of the evening sky. The pale ivory of the tower scintillated mercury green from myriad bits of mica embedded in its sides. Behind it, a fan of blue searchlights splayed out like the rays of an alien sun, rising at dusk. The crowd stopped as one, mouths open, *oohs* and *aahs* sounding all around.

When they reached the tower itself, Polly wanted to examine the material close up and see if she could locate the hidden lamps.

"We'll say our goodbyes, then," Haskel said. "And

stroll on to other marvels." A quick round of goodnight hugs and once again Haskel and Emily split off from their companions and walked together through the fairyland of light.

The Moorish-inspired Court of the Moon lay on the south side of the tower. A bland beige by day, it was breathtaking now, deep blues and pinks creating an orchid glow. From each octagonal corner turret, cutouts in the stone, lit from within, formed golden crescents and stars.

Haskel longed to paint it, to capture the particular quality of the light. It would make a fabulous cover, the subtle interplay of colors, the shapes evocative of far-off lands, simple, magnificent, and otherworldly.

"Golly," Emily said. "This is the best—the best—*Wednesday* of my life."

"Mine too. Our moon. Our stars," Haskel answered, surprising herself. She was not a romantic. "Let's find a place away from the crowds."

They stepped off the path and found a niche around the corner of a wall, hidden by a flowering tree. Haskel pulled Emily close and kissed her, truly kissed her, as if the laws of the city across the water no longer applied. Emily fit her slender body into Haskel's and returned the embrace. For a long moment, surrounded by orchid-tinted shadows and the fragrance of lilacs, they were alone in a garden of unnatural delight.

Emily laid her head on Haskel's shoulder. "This is so nice. I could—"

From the path fifteen feet away, a song broke the spell, a man's voice, loud and off-key. "*Happy days are here again, the skies—*"

"Pipe down," said another man.

"C'mon, Harv. I got three days' leave. I'm gonna see my gal and—"

Haskel stiffened. She craned her head to peek around the lilac branch that hid them from view. "Shit," she said, biting the word off so the sound wouldn't carry.

"What?" Emily pulled away, her face taut with worry.

"Shh. Those sailors," she whispered.

"They can't see us."

"No. But, the lanky dark one on the end?"

"The singing one? He's drunk. What about him?"

Haskel sighed, deep and ragged and weary. "That's Len. That's my husband."

THE FORBIDDEN CITY

They had gotten back from the fair very late, were still sleeping when a loud pounding on the door woke them.

"'Retta! Lemme in!"

Beside her, Emily felt Haskel's body tense.

"Stay here," she whispered into Emily's ear. "Don't make a sound." She got up, put on her tartan robe, and stepped to the hallway door. She did not open it.

"Not a good time, Len. I'm working."

"What kinda how-dee-do's *that*? You got another man in there, darlin'?" He sounded as if he were drunk again. "Tha' why you won' lemme in?"

"No, Len." Haskel took a deep breath. "But I do have a model—posing for a painting—and I'm paying for her time. Come back in an hour."

"Wanna see you *now*." More pounding.

"An hour, Len."

"Wha'm I s'posed to do till then? You got any cash?"

Emily heard the sound of bare feet, the rustle of papers as Haskel rummaged on the table, steps back to the door. "Here's a dollar. Get yourself some coffee and a dough-nut." A soft sound as she slid the bill under the door.

He swore. "Some kinda welcome home." Then there was silence, and finally the sound of heavy footsteps on the marble stairs of the old building.

Haskel returned to the bedroom. "Do me a favor?"

"Sure."

"Get dressed and give me a couple hours? Go to Fong Fong's and have breakfast?"

"Are you throwing me *out*?" Emily heard the indignation in her own voice.

"No, I—"

"You'd just like me away from your bed so you can be alone with your husband?"

"Yes," Haskel said gently. "I need to settle things—once and for all—and I don't want you caught in the middle."

"I already am."

"Please?" Haskel took the pack of Viceroys from the bedside table and lit one with a swift strike of a match against her thumbnail. "If you're here, it will only muddy some already very murky waters."

"How?"

"Divorce papers. If he signs, I'm a free woman. If he sees you, he'll use it as an excuse not to."

Emily thought about that. She blew out a long stream of air, then nodded. "I'll make myself scarce, but—look. I haven't asked—Lord knows I've wanted to—how is it that I'm here, naked as a jaybird—the taste of you still on my lips—and you're someone's *wife*?" She crossed her arms. "What's the story?"

"Fair enough. I left home when I was seventeen and came out here. All the black sheep, right?" Haskel began to pace. "I found where the artists hung out—a bar called the Black Cat. I was tall enough that nobody asked any questions. Len was part of that crowd."

She walked to the window, lit another smoke off the end of the first. "Believe it or not, he was a poet. A good one, too. He'd been published—in *The Atlantic*. That impressed me." She sighed. "I was young, he was handsome. That part's an old, old story."

Haskel was silent, staring out at the courtyard. "He was thirty when we got married; I was barely eighteen. We settled into a fleabag on Union Street with four other people, pooled everyone's money, made a pot of spaghetti last for three days, and drank bootleg wine. After a year, I got a scholarship to art school."

She tapped her ash into a saucer. "By then the Depression had hit. Jobs weren't easy to find and he couldn't keep one. He was *better* than those average Joes, and had to let everyone know it. He'd get fired and go into a blue funk. When I sold my first painting, the chip on his shoulder just got bigger."

"Was he still writing poems?"

"Yes, but no one was interested. One mimeographed rag that paid in copies, not cash. Each rejection, he'd go get plastered, start a fight. Couldn't punch for beans. Spent a night or two in the drunk tank and came home, blaming me."

"Why?"

"I was lowbrow, just a hack, working for the pulps. He was the *real* artist." She tossed the butt into the sink. "But I was supporting us—Len couldn't stand that. He never came *after* me, like Ma. Still, once or twice—" She shook her head. "One morning there was a note: Sorry, angel, off to Portland—or Los Angeles or Chicago—need new experiences, new material. He sold vacuums, hoboed, lumberjacked, got a job on the railroad or as a carny. A few weeks, six months, I'd never hear a word. Nights, I drew lingerie ads for the Emporium and modeled for art classes. I made other friends—Diego and Frida, girls from school. I met Franny. My world got bigger. Then he'd come back, full of stories, dead broke. And it would start all over again." She reached for the bag of coffee. "Truth is, I worked hard, and I was good at what I did. After a while, he stopped even trying."

"Why didn't you divorce him then?"

"People like me don't have lawyers." She poured grounds into the percolator and turned on the hot plate. "And it didn't seem important. I'd moved into this place, was making enough to get by. He wasn't around much. I had a few—*friends*—now and then, mostly kept to myself. It wasn't perfect, but it was all right."

"What changed?" Emily slipped into her dungarees and a crumpled checked shirt—time to take a bundle down to the Chinese laundry. She perched on the edge of the table.

"One day I realized I was tense as a cat—waiting for the knock on the door that would upset my nice orderly life. On guard, like I used to be with Ma. Except I wasn't that girl anymore. I didn't need to hide in the cellar, holding my breath. It was *my* goddamn life." She slapped the table for emphasis. "I met Helen this spring, at one of Franny's dinners. When she started modeling for me, I asked her to file the papers."

"How long since you've seen—him?"

"Three years. Almost four. Not even a postcard."

Emily was quiet, then asked the question that made her stomach dance with fear. "Do you still love him?"

"No." Haskel turned and drew her into a hug. "He's just a stranger I used to know. After today, he'll have *no* claim on me."

"What if he won't sign?"

"I'll throw him out on his ear and wait until November, when the court will declare it *finito*. As far as I'm concerned, it's been over for years. Okay?"

"I think so." Emily let herself soften against Haskel's body, feeling her own heart thumping, Haskel's pendant cool and smooth against her cheek.

"Good. Because right now the best gift you can give me is to disappear until noonish. Let me clean up my old mess without worrying about you."

"I can do that," Emily said, even though she wanted to stay and—what? Defend Haskel's honor? Her presence would only complicate things. Len had the law on his side—she and Haskel didn't. Not at all.

Emily left. She wasn't in the mood for the hordes of teenagers that clustered around Fong Fong's fountain clamoring for "chop suey sundaes," so she bought a paper and went to a café on Columbus. She ordered coffee and toast and did the crossword puzzle with her fountain pen, focusing on forming each letter perfectly, so the ink wouldn't smear, so her mind wouldn't wander back to the studio.

Quarter after eleven, she walked over to Mona's to get the book she'd left in the dressing room. She slipped down the alley and knocked at the stage door, the performers' rap—three short, two long. After a minute, a rough voice said, "Yeah?"

"It's Em—it's Spike."

The door opened. It was Rusty, a tough older woman who did odd jobs and repairs, and sometimes bartended. "C'mon in."

Emily took two steps, blinking in the sudden dimness, and fanned her hand in front of her face. "Jeez-sooey! What died in here?"

"Sewer pipe broke. Believe it or not, it's worse downstairs." Rusty picked up a stack of the silver souvenir folders tourists got when they had their photos taken "with the stars," and stacked them on a shelf in the open supply cupboard. "Mona says we'll be dark tonight and tomorrow."

"Both?"

"City *says* they'll send a crew out this afternoon, but it's gonna take at least another day to air the place out." She held up her hands, a *what-ya-gonna-do* gesture. "If we served food, they'd have closed us down for a week."

"Lucky it's just booze." Emily headed down the narrow hallway to the back room.

"Just a sec," Rusty said. "Package came for you yesterday." She opened a closet and handed her a large, flat box. "Here ya go."

"Thanks." Emily had moved so much it made sense to use the club as a mailing address, but in a year, she'd only gotten a couple of letters and the occasional bill. She looked at the postmark, and the coffee in her stomach rolled like a breaking tide. New Haven, Connecticut. She hadn't heard from her family since Jilly.

She took the box back to the dressing room and laid it on the table, clearing away tins of brilliantine, tubes of pancake makeup, a stack of girlie magazines, and an empty bottle of Four Roses. The return label said **E. Netterfield**, with her parents' address, as if she had shipped something to herself from the past.

"Neddy," she said to herself. She smiled. Edward McCauley Netterfield, her younger brother. Ned, since he'd been old enough to talk. *Father* was Edward. Ned was the only one who hadn't cut ties with her, but he still lived at home. They'd used a mutual friend as a "mail drop," which sounded very Dashiell Hammett, but had allowed her to write to him a few times without their parents' knowledge.

She unwrapped the box and lifted the lid. Inside, on top of an acre of folded tissue paper, was a note in Ned's back-slanted hand:

Sis—

I finally hit that growth spurt Doc Wolfe promised—five inches! None of my glad rags fit, so a gift for that mad act of yours. (I told Mother I gave it to the Salvation Army.) Long letter next month when I become a Princeton man and my mailbox is my own.

Always yours,
Ned

Underneath the tissue was a swallow-tailed coat with satin lapels, white tie, starched shirt front, vest, trousers, gloves, and even a pair of spats. The label in the coat bore the name of New Haven's finest tailor.

Emily whistled through her teeth and checked the clock on the wall. A hair past 11:30. She wanted to try it on, but there wasn't time to get into it and out again before noon; walking back to the studio dressed to the nines would draw more attention than she cared for. Better to model it for Haskel later. *Hmm.* She snapped her fingers.

The drawer marked SPIKE was crammed with junk—makeup, tissues, a roll of Life Savers, a pen, some loose change—and she had to dig to come up with the small white box she sought. She tucked it and her book under the folds of tissue paper and closed the box. With the joy of a plan beginning to hatch, a surprise to tickle Haskel's—fancy—she almost skipped toward the stage door.

"You're in a good mood," Rusty said. She stared at the back sink, monkey wrench in hand. "What was in the box?"

"A secret identity," Emily said. "Good luck with the plumbing."

"Gonna need it. At least *you* get the night off."

Emily took the long way round to the studio—up

Broadway to Kearny, past the narrow copper-domed flat-iron building at Columbus, down that wide diagonal street of cafés, bakeries, and shoe-repair shops until she reached the northwest corner of the Monkey Block, the bulky package tight under her arm.

Church bells were sounding noon mass as she took the stairs to the third floor and walked down the long corridor to the back. She knocked, pro forma, just in case Haskel's now-ex-husband had lingered. When there was no answer, she used her key and let herself in.

"Do *I* have a surprise for you," she said as she stepped through the doorway. "My brother Ned sent me his old—" she stopped, stock-still.

Haskel sat on the floor in the center of a flurry of torn paper, facing the window, her back against a leg of the drafting table, her arms around her drawn-up knees.

Emily set the box down with a thump. "What happened?"

No answer.

"Haskel?"

A small shake of her head. The tumble of blond hair, loosed from its clip, rippled like wheat. Emily tiptoed over, not wanting to startle, knelt down, and put a hand on one trembling shoulder. "Are you all right?"

Another shake of the head, a shrug. Emily saw her grip tighten around her knees. She eased herself to the floor and sat down, stroking Haskel's hair. A flinch, then Haskel turned to face her.

"Jesus," Emily hissed.

One eye was swollen almost shut, the skin below it an angry red. A trickle of blood ran from the corner of her mouth.

"What—?" Emily started, but the answer was obvious. She reached up to the table, found the pack of cigarettes, and held one to the uninjured side of Haskel's mouth, a match hovering. A hand slowly reached up, held it, and inhaled deeply.

"Thanks." It wasn't even a whisper, barely a croak.

Emily scooted as close as she could, a one-armed hug, saying nothing, willing her body to give silent comfort.

When the cigarette had burned almost to Haskel's fingers, Emily took it. "Another?" A nod. Emily shook a fresh one out of the pack and lit it from the smoldering butt of the first, the way she'd seen Haskel do a dozen times. The tip glowed. Emily coughed until her eyes watered.

"Please don't die on me today," Haskel said. There was almost a ghost of a smile in her voice.

"I'll do my best." Emily handed her the cigarette, got up, and drank a glass of water. Once she could breathe again, she found the bourbon under the table's skirt and poured a jelly glass half full. "Here," she said, settling to the floor again. "We're out of St. Bernard dogs and brandy." She wrapped Haskel's fingers around the glass.

Haskel took a long, deep swallow. After a minute, she spoke.

"Son of a mother-fucking bitch."

"That's a start."

Len had come, still drunk from the night before, a twenty-four-hour bender. Yes, he'd tried to kiss her. She'd let him have a peck on the cheek. She'd offered coffee, tried to keep it civil. He sat on the couch, jittery, leg bouncing and tapping nonstop. Why had he come, after so long? A few rounds of "You're my wife, aren't you?" before he got to the money. She was rolling in dough, had to be. He'd seen the magazines on every sailor's bunk. Didn't say it was his *wife* drew that crap, but goddamn it, half of that was his. Only fair. She could see that, right?

Haskel drained the glass, gestured for more.

Things got ugly when she told him it was over. He was the one who always left, shouldn't be a surprise. She brought out the court papers. *Who do you think you are, Miss High and Mighty? Someone else getting what's mine by law?* She uncapped the pen, and then he was standing, yelling, calling her *cunt* and *whore*. It was the news that she didn't *need* him to sign, didn't need him for a god-damn thing anymore—she was yelling then too—that was when he'd slapped her across the face, open-hand, but hard enough to knock her off balance.

Haskel lit another cigarette. "Tell you right now, the villain on my next cover's going to be a dark, lanky bastard."

He'd snatched the papers, ripping them—in half, and half again, then into confetti—throwing them at her in handfuls—*There's your goddamn divorce! Not a chance!*

"I raked his cheek and spit in his eye. I wanted to kill him. Might have, if a neighbor hadn't knocked. Should he call the police? I shouted yes, and that's when Len ran," Haskel finished. "Hightailed it down the stairs. I told Mr. Armanino not to bother, thanked him for his concern. Then I sat down, and waited for you to come home."

For fifteen minutes, Emily had listened. She'd held Haskel's hand, stroked her hair. Hoped it was helping. Her own family didn't touch, or share, or sympathize often. They weren't cold or cruel, just proper and formal, even in private. This role was new to her. No chapter in Emily Post had dealt with the right way to comfort your bruised and trembling lover after her husband had tried to shake her down.

Haskel was the strong one—older, more experienced, tougher—at least from appearances. It hurt to see her like this, her hair straggly, her eyes red, face swollen, no trace of the cool, calm, collected woman she had fallen in love with.

When the second glass was empty and Haskel's story had wound down to muttering, when there was nothing more to say for the moment, Emily led her to bed. She undid her clothes as gently as if she were a scared child, bathed her face with a cool cloth, dabbing at the dribble of blood. Iodine would sting, so that could wait. She got Haskel under the covers, pillow plumped behind her head, and undressed herself. She crawled in, spooning around Haskel's back. Hands on her flat belly, head nestled on a broad shoulder, and when they were settled, Emily began to sing, sweet and low. Sound-kisses, lullabies and spirituals, soft and soothing.

Haskel's breathing finally steadied into sleep. Emily lay quietly beside her all afternoon, drowsing but alert to any change, any sound from outside. By the time Haskel stirred, the room was filled with that rose-gold light. She stood and stretched, wincing as her arm brushed her face. She looked once in the mirror, grimaced, then put on her robe, made her way to the couch. She sat heavily.

"I had a cousin come back from the war," she said. "I was seven or eight. No one said anything, but he was always jumpy, like something might explode at any moment, catch him unaware."

"Shell shock."

"I suppose. That's how I feel right now." She touched

her cheek gingerly. "It was just a slap. But it opened up—"

"—a box full of all the old creepy-crawlies?"

"In spades."

"Want to talk about it?"

"I'm all talked out."

"Okay. I'll clean up a bit." Emily used the whisk broom to sweep up the shreds of paper that littered the floor. "This doesn't—?"

"No. There are other copies. Tomorrow night, Len's ship will be on its way to South America. By the time he gets back, he'll be single, whether he likes it or not." She shook her head. "Poor Len. He's a sad, bitter man on the wrong side of forty, lost in a bottle. I almost feel sorry for him, but he's made his own bed. Now I just want it all behind me. Us."

"So do I." Emily's stomach growled as she emptied the dustpan. She rummaged on the curtained shelf and heated a can of stew on the hot plate. They ate cross-legged on the couch, with bowls and spoons, as if they were children in the nursery, having their tea, high up in the house, warm and safe and separate from all the rest of the world.

They said little. When the window and skylight darkened, Emily turned on the lamp and made cocoa. No milk; she tempered the bitterness with bourbon and sugar. It had been fully night for more than an hour when

Haskel sat up with a start.

"You're late for work," she said.

"Oh. Didn't tell you. We're closed, tonight *and* tomorrow. Busted sewer pipe."

"Ugh." Haskel wrinkled her nose. She turned to put her empty mug on the table and noticed the large box by the door. "What's that?"

"White tie and tails. My brother outgrew his."

"Have you tried it on?"

"No, I was waiting to dazzle you."

"I could use a little of that."

Emily took the box into the bedroom and set up the folding paper screen across the doorway. She'd always complained about how complicated women's clothing was—so many hooks and buttons and laces—but formal menswear was just as bad, if not worse. Stiff layers and studs, suspenders to adjust, spats to fasten, pocket square folded just so. Still, it fit perfectly. When she was nearly done, she opened the small white box and used the bureau mirror and a dab of spirit gum to affix a thin mustache to her upper lip. Its shade matched her hair. "Let's see if this one tickles," she said, sotto voce. She stepped around the screen into the studio.

Haskel looked up, did a double-take, and smiled for the first time since that morning. "Wowza."

"Like it?"

"You are, without a doubt, the handsomest boy of the season." She bit a knuckle, thinking. "I have an outfit—a gift from one of the Emporium buyers, years ago. I've never worn it, there hasn't been an occasion, but—" She sighed. "Too bad. We'd be quite stunning together out on a dance floor."

"Let's. Tomorrow night."

"Are you mad? Where? It's taboo, even at Mona's." She made a face. "The law says *that* would be a—what do they call it? Ah, yes. A lewd and dissolute act. An outrage to public decency."

"Only if it's two women dancing."

"Which, if you've noticed, we—" She stopped, her mouth open in shock and admiration. "You're not think-ing—?"

"Why not?"

"Hmm." Haskel came closer, examining Emily from a few feet away.

"Well?"

"Walk. Across the room."

Emily did, her shoulders back, her hips taut, her feet in a slightly wider stance.

"That's *very* convincing."

"I told you I played all the boys' parts on stage. I watched my brother and his friends when they weren't paying attention."

"You look awfully young."

"I'll take a leaf from Polly's book. Posh accent. Second nature. I grew up around swells."

"With that, you might pass."

"I have, after Mona's, coming home late. Not very often, but the mustache and the walk do keep the mashers away." She laughed. "I disappointed one fancy boy something fierce. He was quite smitten."

"I can see why. Where should we go?"

"Forbidden City? Dining, dancing, big crowds, and far enough from Mona's we won't run into anyone we know."

"Except Helen."

"She'll get a kick out of it."

"You know, so will I. Makeup should cover this." She touched her cheek. It was still red and angry-looking, but the swelling had gone down. "Besides, in the outfit I have in mind, no one's going to be looking at my *face*."

"Haskel! I'm shocked."

"Good. I think a scandalous night is just what the doctor ordered." Haskel leaned down and kissed her.

"Does it tickle?"

"Maybe. Let's go find out."

• • •

With no new assignment yet, Haskel tidied the drafting table, boxing the pastel sticks into groups of reds and blues and greens, putting brushes into one jelly jar, pencils and charcoal sticks into another. She swept the colorful dust and shavings into the wastebasket, stacked sheets of paper and sketchbooks.

When she finished, they took two bags of laundry to Sung Mee, then ate at a nearby luncheonette, hamburger sandwiches and Coca-Colas. Haskel bought two packs of cigarettes at the newsstand at the corner while Emily used the pay phone to check in on the progress at Mona's.

"Still closed," she said when she returned. "The game's afoot."

They went back to the studio. Haskel smoked and sketched Emily, who lay on the couch reading the first issue of *Diabolical Dr. Wu Yang,* "to get into the mood for tonight."

Around six, they went down the hall to shower. In the bedroom, Emily finger-combed her hair, which dried in minutes. Haskel wrapped hers in a towel-turban while she put on makeup. It took both foundation *and* powder to cover the bruise, fading to a dusky lavender at the edges. She lined her eyes with pencil, mascaraed her lashes, and did her full lips in a deep, rich red.

She unwound the turban, combing out her hair, letting

it fall loose to her shoulders, a sleek tawny-gold waterfall with a slight wave.

Emily stared, startled at the transformation. Haskel was a handsome woman but now she was—striking. Stunning.

"You like?" Haskel asked, her throaty voice low. She smiled. "You do." She tilted her head toward the studio. "Dress out there. Let me surprise you."

"You already have. There's more?"

"Wait and see."

"First, I need the mirror to do my—whiskers."

Mustache in place—looking very odd above her own striped bathrobe—Emily gathered her suit and all its various accoutrements and went into the studio. The paper screen slid across the doorway behind her. She heard the sound of the wardrobe opening, a shurring of fabrics and the clatter of wooden hangers, then a soft, "Ah, *there* you are."

It was easier to get into the tails the second time. She almost left her bra off—she was flat-chested enough that it wouldn't matter under the starched layers of shirt and vest and jacket—but remembered the three-garment rule. Bra, panties, and her low-heeled black pumps, all of them with their ladies' shop labels worn but legible. It was a silly law, but better safe than sorry, she thought as she buttoned the spats.

She used a dab of Vaseline to slick her hair into a more masculine style—if they did this again, she'd invest in a tube of Brylcreem—and called, "Ready when you are, Millicent."

The screen slid open and Haskel stepped out.

All Emily could do was whistle.

Haskel wore a midnight-blue jumpsuit of iridescent, shimmery satin that clung to every curve. Padded shoulders, a plunging neckline, and a silver belt at her waist. The sleeves were long and form-fitting, the pants full and flowing, giving the illusion of a skirt. She wore her pendant and two tiny pieces of lapis at her ears.

She looked like a movie star.

"C'mere." Haskel held out a hand and led them back into the bedroom, posing them in front of the mirror inside the wardrobe door.

"You're right," Emily said. "No one's going to pay *me* the slightest attention."

"I'm masquerading just as much as you are."

The evening was warm. They decided to walk. More direct to go down Montgomery, the center of the financial district, but it was gray and shuttered after the close of business. Instead they strolled west, across Washington to Grant and into the heart of Chinatown.

"I love this city," Emily said. From the studio she could walk for ten minutes in one direction and be in an Italian village; in another she'd be on the docks, or in a world of stockbrokers. Every ramble was an adventure.

Grant Avenue was the most colorful and exotic street in a city full of wonders. There be dragons. Lined with pagoda-topped buildings and crimson-coated doorways, every corner blazed with neon signs in English, Chinese, and the curious typographic hodgepodge of the two, spelling out CHOP SUEY, LOTUS ROOM, LI-PO, marketing its otherness.

It was as if a bit of the Orient had been transplanted halfway around the world, making the very sidewalks seem alien. But unlike the exhibits at the fair, it was a real community, a city-within-a-city, the most densely popu-lated square mile in San Francisco.

On a Friday night, the streets were jammed with tourists, mingling with sharp-dressed modern young Chinese and elderly women in drab black. Storefronts selling cheap souvenirs stood next to acrid-smelling shops of pickled fish, dried herbs, and ancient remedies. Brightly lit windows displayed edible marvels: hanging rows of golden roasted ducks, flattened as if starched and ironed; decorated cakes with elaborate icing and elusive flavors; tubs of snails, eels, octopus. Even fruit and veg-etable stands were stacked with colorful, unidentifiable delicacies.

Side streets told another story, glimpses of overcrowded tenements, small dingy shops, laundry hanging from open windows, smells of incense and garbage, garlic and ginger, hot fry-oil and urine.

At the southern end of Grant, just before the huge dragon gates that marked the boundary between this and the ordinary city, the shops were smaller, less flashy. They carried Japanese goods—kimonos, antiques, silk stockings. One store had plywood nailed over a broken window; red paint in dripping letters said NO JAP GOODS! An adjacent store had a neatly printed sign on its door: BOYCOTT SILK. BE IN STYLE, WEAR LISLE. Japan and China had been at war for a decade. The protests had appeared after the massacre at Nanking.

Emily and Haskel walked through the dragon gates, crossed Bush Street. One block farther was Sutter. They turned the corner. The two-story neon column for Forbidden City bathed the stone walls of an otherwise unremarkable commercial block in green, red, and gold light.

Sedans and taxis queued in front of the building. A uniform-clad doorman ushered well-dressed couples through bright scarlet double doors ornamented with gold medallions.

"Walter, are you sure this is *safe*?" asked a woman in a silver gown.

"It's fine, dear. It's not like we're *in* Chinatown."

The doorman gave a small bow to Emily and held the

door for Haskel. They climbed the stairs, lined with silk hangings and brush-and-ink paintings, to the second-floor lobby. Its bamboo-paneled walls held more Oriental decor, interspersed with framed photos of Hollywood celebrities who had visited the nightclub. To their left was a long bar, already four deep with customers.

"We'll never get a seat," Haskel said.

Emily pitched her voice low for the benefit of the people around them. "Now, don't you worry your pretty little head," she said, patting Haskel's arm. She stepped up to the tuxedoed maitre d'. "Fitzbottom. Table for two."

He looked down at a list. "Very good, sir. Right this way." He led them through the round moon-gate entrance to the club itself and pulled out a chair at one of the floor-side tables. "Madam." Haskel sat and he returned to his station.

"How did you pull *that* off?" she asked, smiling.

"The call from the newsstand."

"Will wonders never cease?"

They sat on the rim of the dance floor, facing the stage, its red velvet curtains closed. Behind them rose two horseshoe tiers of tables. The room was full, nearly three hundred people; except for the staff, everyone was white.

A waiter in a red silk uniform and tasseled cap came by with menus and took their drink orders. "Gin fizz for the lady?"

Haskel shook her head. "Bourbon on the rocks."

The right side of the menu offered Chinese dinners—all of them variations on chop suey and egg fu yeong. The American side boasted fried chicken, steaks, and chops. Either dinner cost a dollar, including a relish tray and dessert.

"Fried chicken, the international delicacy," Emily said. They each ordered a steak. The meals came on platters with silver domes that the waiter removed with a polished flourish.

Haskel cut into her meat. "I could get used to this."

"You'll have to paint faster, then. This one's my treat—Ned left a tenner in the suit pocket—but my piggy bank doesn't rattle much."

"Your Ned is a sweet boy."

"He is indeed."

They'd finished their supper and ordered a second round of drinks when the curtains parted and a short, dapper Chinese man stepped out.

"Welcome to the Forbidden City," he said into the microphone. "I am your Celestial host, Charlie Low. Tonight you'll enjoy a new *slant* in entertainment." He beamed and waited for the chuckles to subside. "We have singers, dancers, every kind of show you want. I don't know about you, but a couple of Wong numbers sound right to me!" More laughter. "So please, welcome to the stage, the Chinese Ethel Merman, Miss Dorothy Chow!"

A well-built young woman came out in a sequined gown. The band struck up a tune, and she began to belt out "I Got Rhythm." Her voice was strong and sure and would have reached to the back tier of seats even without a mike.

"Nice vibrato," Emily whispered. From behind them, she heard a woman say, shrill and inconsiderately loud, "Harry! She sings just like a white girl!"

Haskel made a face. "And tomorrow, they'll go to the aquarium to see the trained seals."

The next act was a magician, demonstrating the Mysterious Secrets of the Far East, the Chinese Harry Houdini. Following him were "those Oriental Rug-cutters, the Chinese Fred and Ginger—Eddie and Helen Young!"

Helen wore a flowing pale green gown with a full skirt that billowed when she twirled around her partner in his sleek black tuxedo. They did a slow rumba to "Begin the Beguine," moving elegantly, effortlessly to the Cole Porter tune until the band began an up-tempo rhythm. In one fluid motion, Helen tore away her skirt to reveal a pair of green satin shorts, her shapely legs clad in fishnet stockings.

She and Eddie began to tap-dance, their feet a syncopated accompaniment to the music. The dance grew more and more physical as Eddie did a backflip and Helen leapt over him, landing in a full splits, all in rhythm, never missing a beat. The audience's applause was long and loud.

The emcee stepped up again. "Now, we have an act you won't see anywhere else. You know what they say about Chinese girls—down there?" He leered genially at the audience.

A soldier to Emily's left said, "Hey, Ralphie, what's he mean?"

His buddy replied in a loud whisper, "Don' you know nothin', Pat? They got slanted pussies, too. Goes from side to side, not front to back."

"That so?"

"Yep. Like eatin' corn on the cob."

The emcee had continued his introduction throughout the crude soldier's explanation, and announced, "The Chinese Sally Rand!" The lights dimmed and a diffused pink spot highlighted a beautiful young girl, naked except for silver high heels. She held a translucent balloon a yard in diameter, walking and turning so that there was never more than a partial glimpse of her body.

Half the men in the room were on their feet, clapping and shouting. The dancer lifted the bubble over her head for a brief second before the stage went dark and the curtain closed. As the applause died down, the band began playing "Dancing Cheek to Cheek," and couples got up from their tables and headed to the dance floor.

"May I have this number?" Emily stood and held out her hand, a grin playing at the corner of her mouth.

"Let me check my dance card," Haskel replied. "Ah, I have an open spot. Do you know how to lead?"

"Fifteen years of girls' schools? I can manage." She took Haskel's arm and led her onto the floor, put a hand at the small of her back, and twirled her expertly. For the next ten minutes, the world fell away. There was nothing but the music, satin on skin, warm breath on a cheek. They danced, holding each other close, even kissing once, as if they were an ordinary couple. No one stared. No one paid the slightest attention. Emily had never felt so happy. She tilted her head up and was about to be kissed again when a nearby voice said softly, "Haskel?"

Emily's grip tightened. She turned them slowly and let out a sigh of relief when she saw it was Helen, wearing a tight *cheongsam*, deep green with gold embroidery, a long slit up the side. She wore heavy makeup that emphasized the shape of her eyes.

"Who's your fella—?" Helen's mouth opened in surprise. "Well, butter my butt and call me popcorn!" She shook a scolding finger at them. "It's not what I think, huh?"

"It wasn't—then," Emily replied. "Come back to our

table. Don't you showgirls let the fellows buy you drinks?"

"That's the idea. We're supposed to dance with them, too, but—"

"That's okay. I'll pass." They all sat down.

"What on god's green earth are you two doing?" Helen asked after the waiter had taken drink orders and the cigarette girl had come and gone.

Haskel smiled. "Seeing how the other half lives." She pointed to the stage. "Some of that must be pretty hard to take."

"The slant-eye crap?" Helen shrugged. "It's what the tourists come for. You learn to roll with the punches." She saw the doubt on her friend's face. "Look, it's Hollywood and *your* magazines that sell all that Yellow Peril, Fu Manchu stuff. These folks have bought into it hook, line, and sinker. They come here to be titillated and terrified, expecting the depraved Dragon Lady in her opium den. Instead they get show tunes and some pretty good dancing."

"Pretty good? You and Eddie were outstanding."

"Thanks. So maybe a couple of rubes go home believing a girl like me can do more than cook noodles and washee-washee laundry." She made a face. "Are Charlie's jokes funny? No. But I get paid to dance and Dottie gets to sing. Unless it was some bullshit *ching-chong* sing-song, dressed up like little fragile dolls, no place else would hire us."

"Like Jack at Mona's," Emily said.

"Pretty much. All of *us* are fantasies to them. Sexy and exotic." She laughed. "Hah. Exotic Coos Bay. *That why I speekee pretty good English, you bet!*" She drained her drink. "What the hell, it pays the bills." The house lights blinked on and off. "Time for act two. I need to go change."

Emily looked around. "Where's the dressing room? We didn't see any performers on the way in."

"You wouldn't. It's up the stairs from the alley, out back." She stood, waved to another girl, and disappeared down a hallway behind the bandstand.

The second show was similar, but not identical, to the first. Acrobats replaced the magician, Charlie made different "yellow" jokes, and the Chinese Ethel Merman belted out "Anything Goes." Helen and Eddie jitterbugged to Benny Goodman's "Stompin' at the Savoy," and nearly brought down the house.

Haskel and Emily danced during the next interval. "How 'bout we stay here forever, just like this?" Emily murmured into Haskel's neck.

"I'd rather go home and find out what's under that starched shirt of yours."

"Nothing you haven't seen before."

"I'd like to see it again. Besides, you don't need any-thing more to drink."

"'Tis true." When the song ended, she took Haskel's hand. "Let us weave our way homeward."

Out in the lobby, a line of people waited to get in for the late show. They squeezed by and went downstairs.

"Did you have a pleasant evening, sir?" the doorman asked.

"Extremely." Emily tipped a finger to her temple in what she hoped was a posh salute.

A dozen people stood on the sidewalk, waiting for their rides or trying to flag a taxi on the busy one-way street. "Friday night, Grant's going to be a circus," Haskel said. "Let's go up Stockton and walk through the tunnel."

They'd gone about thirty feet when, out of the shad-ows of a shuttered storefront, stepped a man in sailor's blues, his round cap low on his forehead, his left cheek striped with three raised welts.

"I *knew* there was another guy," he shouted. "You lyin' bitch!"

"Len!" Haskel's voice cracked in surprise. "What are—?"

"Followed from your place. But the Chink in the mon-key suit wouldn't let me in the damn door." He took a swig from the neck of a bottle protruding from a paper bag wadded in his fist. His voice was loud enough that two people in front of the nightclub turned to see what the commotion was.

Emily took Haskel's arm. "Let's go back. We'll get a cab."

"No you don'. You're not going anywhere with *my* wife." He reached for Haskel's other arm.

She pulled away toward the building behind her.

Without thinking, Emily stepped between them. She lowered the timbre of her voice and growled, "Stay away from her."

"Yeah? You gonna *make* me, rich boy?" Len put his fists in the air, pistoning them back and forth like a cartoon boxer.

Emily raised her own hands. She didn't want to fight, but she'd scrapped with boys before and knew how to defend herself. At least she used to.

Len swung, a big roundhouse that barely grazed her sleeve. He spun halfway around with the momentum, and dropped the paper bag. It hit the cement with a wet *pop*!

"*Now* see whad'ya made me do!" he yelled. He turned, his eyes wild, and swung again. Emily pivoted, taking most of the weak blow on her shoulder, and caught his wrist. She thrust him away using his arm as leverage.

Len stumbled backward. His foot hit the edge of the curb and twisted under him. Arms flailing, unable to regain his balance, he fell into the street. A Yellow Cab, its light off, barreled west down Sutter. Brakes squealed, too late. It clipped Len in mid-tumble.

He flew over the taxi's hood and landed on the asphalt. He lay sprawled, still. A red stain began to spread across his white cap.

Time stopped.

Emily and Haskel stood on the sidewalk in shock.

Two buildings over, the crowd began to react.

A woman screamed.

"That young guy hit him. Knocked him right into the street," said a man.

The doorman blew his whistle, three sharp bursts.

"Len." Haskel stared, her hand to her mouth.

"I didn't—" Emily started.

"I know." Haskel's face was pale. She looked into the street, closed her eyes. Then she took a deep breath. "Go find Helen. Change back into a girl, fast."

"I can't just *leave* you—"

"I'm his wife. The cops *will* find me. It's better if I wait here." Haskel pointed in the direction of Stockton Street, away from the nightclub entrance. "Go. Now. Before the cops get here."

"I've got three garments on."

"It won't be *vice* that's coming, Em. If they get a hold of you—" She shuddered. "You know how they treated Big Jack."

"Yes. Okay." Emily began to walk. She looked back over her shoulder. "Where do I—?"

"Franny's. I'll come when I can. Just *go*."

Peeling off the mustache, Emily continued to the corner. She moved slowly, as naturally as she could. She wanted to break into a run. She wanted to go back and put her arms around Haskel and never let go. She wanted to turn the clock back a hour, so none of this ever happened. Instead she strolled to the mouth of the alley. It was dark except for a pool of light spilling down from an open door on the second floor, where a young Chinese man lounged in his trousers and under-shirt, smoking.

Emily climbed the stairs. "Helen Young? It's an emergency."

He looked her up and down, then stepped aside to let her in. "She's dressing," he said. "I'll get her."

Helen appeared a minute later in a thin robe. "What's wrong?"

"Everything. Haskel's—" Emily trembled as she gave her the short version. "The cops will be looking for a man in tails. I need to ditch this suit and borrow other clothes."

"Come with me." Helen took her back to the women's dressing room, raising a few eyebrows from the chorus girls who were changing for their last number. "Auditions at Mona's," Helen explained. That got two nods, a smile, and a wink.

Helen's clothes were too small; a taller girl named Patsy loaned her a dress. "I'll walk home in my costume," she said. "It's only four blocks."

Ten minutes later, Emily stood in front of the mirror, goggling at herself. She wore a green dress with a pleated skirt, a beige cardigan, and a string of pearls. Helen had used makeup to age her a few years, applied lipstick in a subtle shade of red, and toweled the Vaseline out of her hair, fluffing it to give her a soft halo of curls. She added a brown hat with a pale gold feather. "There. You could walk into a tea room in Pacific Heights and no one would look twice. No one will recognize you."

"Including me," Emily said. Only the shoes were her own.

She looked nothing like the young man who had fought with Len.

She looked nothing like Spike.

What was unsettling was that she didn't look like Emily, either.

A girl who dressed as a boy, disguised as a woman.

"Breathe," Helen said. "I'll hang up your suit with the men's costumes." She patted Emily's shoulder. "I'm done for the night. I'll put on my street clothes and go wait with Haskel. If it's as bad as you think, this could take all night, and it wouldn't hurt for her lawyer to be present."

"Thanks," Emily said. Her voice was barely audible. She was numb, as if this was all a bad dream. Nothing felt real.

"Eddie'll walk you over to the St. Francis. There'll be people around, and you can catch the Powell-Hyde cable car. Get off at Green. It's only a couple of blocks to Franny's. I'll phone from here, let them know you're coming."

"Glad someone can still think," Emily stood and hugged Helen. "Thank you."

"People like us, we help each other." She walked her to the back stairs.

Eddie took her arm as if she were his date, and escorted her down the alley. They took Post Street over to Union Square, and stood across from the elegant entrance to the St. Francis Hotel until the cable car arrived. Emily got on, paid her fare, and watched behind her as the car climbed slowly up the steep grade of Nob Hill, its bell clanging, and the rest of the world disappeared into the fog.

TUNDÉRPÖR

Haskel called from a pay phone a little before ten the next morning. Franny answered. Yes, Haskel said, they'd questioned her all night, first a beat cop on the curb, then a pair of homicide detectives down at the station. Too many witnesses willing to swear it wasn't an accident. "Let me talk to Em."

"Where are you? Are you okay?"

"I'm tired. They let me go half an hour ago."

"What did you tell them about—"

"The other fellow? As little as I could." Haskel's voice was hoarse and she was exhausted. She lit a cigarette, exhaled. "That he'd asked me to dance and we struck up a conversation. He lived somewhere down the peninsula. I didn't get his name. He was a gentleman, walked me out to hail a cab when—" Long pause. "Cops didn't like that at all—a married woman picking up a man at a night club."

"I'm so sorry," Emily said. "I shouldn't have—"

"Defended yourself? And me? Look, Len didn't deserve what happened, but he did swing first. The rest was a stupid, goddamn accident. No one to blame." There was a long pause, static crackling on the line. Haskel imagined Emily's face, her hands white-knuckled around the black receiver. "I love you," she said. She never thought she'd say *that* again. Hell of a time.

"Me too," Emily whispered. "I'll be there in twenty minutes."

"No, stay put. Two of the witnesses were sober enough to give decent descriptions of the young guy who threw the punch. There'll be a sketch in the afternoon papers."

"I want to see you."

"Tonight, I'll want that more than anything, but right now I need a stiff drink or two and some sleep. I'll call when I can think straight."

"After I get off work, then."

"Mona's," Haskel said. "Damn, damn, damn." She blew a cloud of smoke, filling the inside of the phone booth.

"What?"

"The papers. If the sketch is any good—"

"—someone might recognize Spike, and the jig'll be up." Emily sighed, deep and long. "Alright. I'll call Mona from here. Laryngitis. Always a good excuse for a singer. Might be a few days, the doctor says."

"Good thinking. By then this'll be yesterday's news."

Emily hung up the phone, but before she could dial Mona's number, there was a knock downstairs.

"It's like Grand Central Station," Babs said. She went

down to see who it was, and came up a minute later with Helen. The dancer's face was pale, dark circles under her eyes. She slumped onto the couch.

"Coffee?" Franny asked. "Something stronger?"

"Both," Helen said. "There's a problem."

"Christ, now what?" Franny poured a cup of coffee and added a jigger of brandy.

"The cops *might* have a link between Mona's and the 'young man' Haskel was with." She frowned. "Imagine the headlines. *Deviant Wanted in Sailor's Death*. That'd sell some papers."

"How? Oh—" Emily snapped her fingers. "The dressing room."

Helen nodded. "One of the girls told Charlie Low. I don't know if he passed it on to the cops, but we've got to assume they'll be watching both clubs."

"Shit," Franny said.

"On a shingle."

Emily walked over to the window and stared out at the bay, the same deep blue as the sky, today. She watched a ship steaming toward one of the piers, its wake a frothy white, and made a decision.

"I can't let Mona or Mickey or the other girls get hurt." She turned. "Can I use the phone?"

Mona wouldn't be at the club yet, not this early. Emily dialed her at home. "Mona? It's Spike. Sorry for no notice, but it's my sister in Los Angeles. Her baby's coming—a month early. Uh-huh." She listened, drumming her fingers, then responded. "No, I'm at the train station now. I'll be gone a week, maybe two." More drumming. "Really? Gladys Bentley's singing *there*? Sure. I'll try." She nodded. "Thanks. You're a peach." She hung up the phone.

"That will buy you some time," Franny said.

"And throw the cops off the scent. If anyone at Mona's recognizes you from the papers, they'll say you're down south." Helen drained her coffee and held out the cup for a refill.

The phone was silent for a few hours. When it rang, late that afternoon, Babs got up from the kitchen table, where the five of them sat around a plate of crackers and cheese and Italian salami, barely nibbling.

"Haskel's awake," she said to Emily. "She'd like us to send you home." She returned to the table. "Besides us, who knows you're staying there?"

"No one. I use the club as my address, and as far as the other girls know, I'm still rooming at Big Jack's."

"Good." She cut a slice of Gouda. "The papers will be on every newsstand by now. We need to get you into the studio without being seen." She looked over at Franny and raised an eyebrow in question.

"I prepared one yesterday," Franny said. "Fortunately it was foggy last night."

"Prepared what?" Polly asked.

"A temporary short cut."

"Franny's a—" Helen groped for an acceptable word, failed. "Apologies. My brain's a bit fogged with lack of sleep." She shrugged. "—A sort of witch."

"Hrumph. I am a woman of exceptional abilities."

Polly frowned. "You're all pulling my leg."

"Not at all, child. There are—powers—that run in our family. It is—" She stopped and shook her head. "It is a conversation you and I will have to have in some depth, but not right now."

She went over to a shelf and picked up a small red paper bird, folded in sharp angles, handing it to Emily. "The short cut. Just before you get to the end of the lane, pull the wings gently outward." She circled each thumb and index finger and mimed. "When you're safely inside the studio, burn it and blow the ash out the window."

"Right," said Emily. "Thank you." She stifled a smile. Franny and her hocus-pocus. "You're good friends," she added, feeling ungracious, and kissed her on the cheek.

Opening the front door, she stepped out into the shadow of the enormous banyan tree whose branches nearly covered the length of Caligo Lane. She walked two houses west, stopping just short of the street. "Okay. Magic trick, take one," she said under her breath. She pulled the paper wings and turned the corner.

"Holy Joe! It—" Emily was not on Jones Street, not on Russian Hill at all, but at the intersection of Montgomery and Washington, at the rear door of Haskel's building, nearly a mile from Franny's. She walked up the back stairs in disbelief, her heart pounding, gripping the tiny bird with shaking hands.

She knocked on the studio door with an elbow, afraid of letting go of the paper wings.

Haskel opened it, wrapped Emily in a hug. "You look different."

"You noticed." She looked down at the pleated dress and cardigan. "I need a match."

"What?"

"Franny." She held up the bird. "She really *is* a—"

"Yes. It's startling the first time, isn't it?"

"I'll say." Emily lay the tiny sculpture on the windowsill. She lit one edge and watched until it was no more than a pile of gray ash, then blew gently. It drifted out over the courtyard in the warm summer breeze.

They sat on the couch and held each other for what could have been hours—or moments—each murmuring about how glad she was the other was safe. Emily finally stood and stretched, heading for the bedroom. "I need to change into my own clothes."

Haskel followed. "How about no clothes?"

"That would be even better."

It was dark when Haskel went out to buy sandwiches and a jug of wine. They picnicked on the floor, filling each other in on the events of the last twenty-four hours.

"You can't risk being seen. What are you going to do, cooped up here for a week or two?"

Emily thought. "Work on a story, maybe."

"Will I be in it?"

"You'll have to wait and see." She poured more wine. "You?"

"Not sure. Start a new painting, at least make some sketches."

"Monsters?"

"No. Seeing Len like that put me right off horror. Landscapes. Or nudes." She smiled. "If only I had a model."

Late the next morning Haskel went out for raspberry rings and the Sunday *Chronicle*. The sketch was startlingly accurate, mustache and all, but was buried on page four. Emily read the book reviews and did the acrostic, Haskel critiqued the drawing style of the funnies. They tried to pretend they were an ordinary couple on an ordinary weekend, and nearly succeeded.

The illusion was shattered early Monday afternoon with a knock on the door. Haskel stiffened, and motioned Emily into the other room. "If it's the cops, hide inside the wardrobe," she whispered.

It wasn't. It was Helen. She was in her lawyer suit, holding a briefcase, and her face was grim.

"What's wrong?" Haskel asked.

"You might want to sit."

Haskel sat. Emily stood in the bedroom doorway.

"They're stymied, down at the station, no leads on the mystery man, just crazies calling in. They've got plain-clothes watching the train station and Greyhound."

"You said they would." Haskel lit a cigarette. "How long will they keep it up?"

"No idea. But now the feds are involved."

"*What*? Why?"

"Len's—estate. The skinny detective, Compton, said they requested a background check on him Friday night. Routine procedure. Weekend, though, so no response. Now it's Monday, and a federal beef came in over the wire. Income tax. Len hadn't paid a dime since '34. With penalties and fines, he was in the hole almost two grand."

"Jesus."

"Yeah, and here's the kicker. You were legally married when he died, so you're on the hook for every cent of it."

"Hold on. I paid *my* taxes. I have the records."

"Last time he filed, he checked married, jointly. The form has his signature—and yours."

"Son of a bitch!" Haskel sputtered. "It's a forgery."

"I'm sure it is. And you *might* be able to prove it in

court. The fact that you'd already filed for divorce could work in your favor. It might also look like you were trying to weasel out of paying. Depends on the judge." She set her briefcase down. "You've got a few weeks before they'll close probate. I'll try and find you a good tax lawyer."

"Who'll be expensive."

"Yep." Helen looked around. "I don't suppose you have enough to—?"

"Not even close. I've got maybe three hundred cash in a coffee can at the top of the closet. And the magazines owe me for two covers, that's another one-eighty."

"Which Uncle Sam can garnish as soon as the checks clear."

"Shit." Haskel lit another cigarette off the end of the first. "So assuming you find me a halfway decent lawyer—?"

"I could get you Clarence Darrow—if he wasn't dead—and your chances in court would still be slim to none, under the circumstances." Helen pointed at the pack of smokes. "Give me one of those." She lit up. "Okay, worst-case scenario. The cops uncover your—unsavory—lifestyle. Then they find out who your dance partner really was, and things get very ugly, very fast." She ticked them off on her fingers. "Lying in a homicide investigation, obstruction of justice, lewd public behavior. The papers would have a field day. You'd both be looking at jail—maybe prison—and your story would be on the cover of *Spicy Detective* in time for Christmas."

Haskel swore. "Sugarcoat it, why don't you?"

"Sorry. Rock and a hard place. You have anywhere else to go?"

"What do you mean?"

"Well, the beat cops aren't watching the bus station for *you*. Leave town, change your name, wait for things here to settle down."

"And leave Em to the wolves? No."

"I figured. For what it's worth, I wouldn't either. So now we work on Plan B."

"Which is?"

"I haven't got a goddamn clue."

• • •

After Helen left, Haskel and Emily sat on the couch. Haskel smoked. Neither of them spoke. Finally Emily said, "Damn it, I really liked this story. But it doesn't seem to be ending well." She laid her head on Haskel's chest, feeling the muscles rigid with tension. "Maybe you *should* go away, just for a little while."

"Looking over my shoulder every second?" Haskel

shivered. "No. I won't hide. Never again."

"Okay then. Plan B. Could Franny—?" She groped for the words. "—escape us somewhere?"

"I don't think so. I asked her once. She said she's never managed a—short cut—farther than a mile or so. She and Babs are trying to figure out a way for her to maybe, someday, work long-distance, but it's—complicated." She held up her hands. "Maps and scale and ratios. They were excited; I understood one word in three. Besides, she said a big—jump—could take *months* to calculate. Apparently it's a very precise kind of—"

"Magic?"

Haskel smiled, just a little. "You've become a believer?"

"No. Yes. I don't know. That little bird was rather convincing."

"Keep an open mind then," Haskel said. "I have another Plan B. Plan C, if you like." She stood, facing the couch, as if she were about to give a lecture. "Remember I said my grandmother gave me her old family recipe for *tundérpör*?"

Emily nodded. "And a bus ticket and your necklace. But even if I am always hungry, I don't think cooking is going to help."

"*Tundérpör* isn't food."

For the first time since they'd met, Haskel undid the

clasp of her pendant and took it off. She pushed on the blue stone with both thumbs, hard; after a moment, it popped out of its setting into her palm. "This is *tundérpör*. Or will be very soon."

"What does *tundérpör* mean? 'Magic rock'?"

"Sort of," Haskel said. "Not exactly." She lit a third cigarette. "One night, after lots of wine, I asked Franny to look it up. By the end of the evening there were dozens of her old books on the table, and the closest she could come was 'pixie dust.' Franny made a face and tossed *that* book into the rubbish. Seems *tundérpör* doesn't really have a—parallel—outside the old country. It's a kind of magic even *she*'d never heard of."

"Wait. Your grandmother's a bigger—you know—than *Franny*?"

"Maybe not bigger. But different."

"Still frightening. What does the rock *do*?"

"Opens a doorway."

She took the mortar and pestle she used to crush the fish glue, wiped both clean with a damp dish towel, and lay the stone in the bottom of the ceramic bowl. She set it on the table and picked up a razor blade. "Give me your finger."

Emily tucked both hands into her pockets. "Not until you explain."

"I'm going to grind a very special pigment. I'll use it

in a painting, and it will—" She faltered. "—It will put *us* into the picture. Then we'll be—" She thought for a minute. "—in another story."

"Wait, what? We're going to be trapped *inside* a painting?"

"No. Think of it as an intersection. A place to change directions." Haskel tapped the razor on the edge of the sink. "My bubbe used *her tundérpör* to escape a pogrom. She was only sixteen, pregnant with my father. She made a little painting, put it in a locket, and—presto—she was in America, somehow. Everyone else in her village was slaughtered."

"Are you part of your—bubbe's—story?"

"Of course. She's my *grand*mother."

"No, I mean—are you inside her magic—?"

Haskel shrugged. "I don't know, Em. Like Franny said, these things have their own rules. That doesn't mean I under*stand* them." She sighed. "Bubbe gave me a recipe, not a textbook."

Emily stood in silence, gazing out the window. "I'm not convinced yet," she said finally. "But what's the first step?"

"I need a drop of your blood, and a drop of mine." She saw the look on Emily's face. "Sorry. Bubbe said that's how it works."

"Our grandmothers would *not* have gotten along," Emily said. "You first."

"Sissy." Haskel pricked the pad of her left index finger, grimacing a little, and squeezed a single drop into the mortar. "There. Your turn."

"I almost pledged a sorority, but they went in for this sort of thing. Secret rituals of Pi Gamma Nu." She reached for the blade. "Are you sure about this?"

"Not entirely. Maybe my bubbe is a crazy old woman who tells tall tales. But what do we have to lose?"

"Point taken." Emily touched the razor to her finger. "Do you have Band-Aids?"

"Yes. *Poke.*"

Emily shut her eyes and poked. "Ow!" The blood welled up as Haskel moved the mortar underneath and caught a fat drop. She handed Emily a tissue.

"Anything more? Eye of newt?"

"Just some spit," Haskel said, still holding the mortar.

"Your grandmother—" Emily spit and Haskel did the same.

She put the mortar down and selected a stick of pale blue pastel chalk, breaking it in half on the edge of the table with a sharp *snap!*, dropping the pieces into the mortar. She began to grind the "ingredients" together. The pendant's stone was unyielding; the tendons in her forearms stood out with the effort, the pestle making a sound like bones dragged across gravel.

Sucking on her punctured finger, Emily leaned against

the windowsill. "Are there magic words?"

"They come later," Haskel said through clenched teeth. She felt the stone crack, and then crack again, and finally begin to pulverize. "*This* is also a rather complicated process." She ground the powder for another five minutes. "There. That ought to be about right." She set the bowl down and rubbed her arm. "It needs to sit overnight."

"Then what?"

Haskel smiled. "For seven years, I've painted other people's fantasies. Tomorrow, I'm going to paint ours."

Emily stared at the blank paper on the drafting table, at the bowl of bluish powder beside it. "How long will we be, um—*in* this new story?"

"Until the painting is destroyed."

"Then what?"

"We wink out, I suppose," Haskel said. "Everyone does. One day you just stop being. Maybe you know it's coming, maybe you don't."

"Like Len."

Haskel nodded. "Len's story just *ended*. No warning." She gave Emily a hug. "Ours will too, someday. Bubbe was almost sixty when I left home. I'd take that."

"So—what if the painting *isn't* destroyed?"

They looked at each other. Haskel lit a cigarette, stared out the window, then turned back and said, her voice low,

"I'll be happy if I can spend the rest of my life with you. But nothing should be *forever*. We're human. We're mortal. It's part of the package."

"Good. That's what I was thinking. I've read a *lot* of stories in those magazines the last two weeks," Emily gestured to the bookcase. "Wanting to be immortal is like playing god—it *never* ends well."

"Nope. It's unnatural."

"Unnatural love still okay?" Emily chuckled.

"More than okay." Haskel kissed her. "I want to grow old with you—twenty, thirty years—rocking chairs and wrinkles and all."

"Twenty years—that's more than a thousand Wednesdays." Emily thought for a minute. "We'll need to figure out a way to protect it—and a safe place to store it."

"A frame, or a box with a glass lid would keep it from getting wet."

"Or nibbled." Emily shivered.

"Ugh. I'll need to know what size so I can trim the paper."

"Maybe Franny can spare one of her old map cases?"

"Perfect."

"But where do we *put* it? How do we know someone won't find it and keep it. What if—?"

"Don't overthink it. We're talking about magically transporting the two of us into a painting that illustrates another story. That doesn't really lend itself to logic."

"Thanks, *that* was reassuring."

"Franny's bird, Em. Remember Franny's bird." Haskel put on her shoes. "I'll go down to the corner and call her now."

· · ·

At noon the next day, Babs, Franny, and Polly came by with Chinese dumplings and spareribs, and a shallow, felt-lined box about the size of a *LIFE* magazine. It had a hinged lid, dark wood framing a sheet of thick glass.

"That's just what we need," Haskel said. She picked up a ruler and began to measure the interior, jotting the dimensions on a piece of scrap paper.

"What happens once it's done?" Emily asked. "If this works, *we* won't be here anymore, but the open box will be."

"I'll take care of that," Franny said. "I've talked to Babs and Helen. How would you feel if we—the rest of us—came in and closed it up, then put it where it won't be disturbed?"

"Please don't bury it." Emily shuddered.

"No, no, dear. I know a place where it will remain hidden. I own a building in Chinatown. Lots of storage space. We'll make sure it stays safe, and we'll be its guardians for the rest of *our* lives. We've agreed to take an oath. Last woman standing will make sure it's destroyed."

"Which will release *us*," Haskel said, nodding. "Are you certain? That's a long commitment."

"I hope so. I'm the eldest, and I'd very much like to see eighty." She winked. "*That* should give the two of you a lovely extended honeymoon."

Haskel kissed Franny on the cheek. "Thank you. It's—above and beyond."

"The Circle is a fierce tribe. We look out for each other. On the other hand, things do change, and we live in *very* uncertain times, as Polly well knows. So it seemed prudent to discuss other contingencies."

"Plan B's Plan B," Emily said.

"Indeed. Circumstances might wrest the painting from our control—"

"So I shall booby-trap it," Polly announced. "If a stranger finds it, they'll be in for a surprise."

They all turned to look at her. Haskel said, "How? What?"

"Well—" Polly tapped a finger on the box. "I started thinking last night, and looked through some of Franny's books. Really, quite an exceptional library. I considered explosives—black powder, or perhaps a combination of sulfur and potassium chlorate. They make a lovely bang when combined." She frowned. "But that does require a strong compressive force, which we can't rely on, and *could* accidentally be detonated during transport."

Babs patted her shoulder. "So nice to have another scientist around." Emily and Haskel just stared.

"However," Polly continued, "since we don't know how *long* a period the trap should be viable, I was forced to re-examine my parameters. The substance might need to remain potent for several decades, without causing any damage to the painting. So—inert, non-corrosive, inflammable. That eliminated anything acidic or pyrotechnic. Then I remembered the medium, the pastels. They're—" she thought for a moment. "Friable, yes? Unless a fixative is applied."

"Very. I use fish glue—isinglass—to stabilize the finished piece."

"*Eau de pêche*," Emily said.

Polly nodded. "Odd, but effective. However, if you omit that step, I have a corker. Organic, won't lose efficacy, and its reactivity is nearly foolproof."

"Can you get your hands on this miracle stuff in the next few days?"

"I have some with me." She tapped her satchel and laughed when Emily took a step back. "Don't worry. It's quite a harmless powder, when used correctly."

"Then do continue, professor." Haskel reached for her smokes.

"Franny and I chose this particular box because at first glance, it appears solid. The hinges are on the interior. I can replace them with spring-loaded ones, then incise three shallow troughs around the lower perimeter, to hold the powder. Before we close the box, I'll apply a thin coat of rubber cement on the underside of the lid to make a tight seal. By camouflaging the latching mechanism, I can render it invisible to all but the *very* closest of inspections."

"Someone leaning right over the box."

"Exactly. If they do manage to trip the latch, the force of the springs will break the seal and release a rather penetrating cloud of—" she pulled out a small red tin and held it up in a dramatic gesture. "Pepper!"

"Ah-choo!" Emily mimicked an enormous sneeze.

"Precisely."

"Poof!" Haskel clapped her hands. "So long, painting."

Emily gave Polly a spontaneous hug. "You're brilliant, you know."

She ducked her head, visibly pleased by the praise. "I'm a Wardlow. It's what we do."

Polly took the box home to tinker with it. Haskel trimmed the paper and pinned it to the drafting table. She lay on the couch, sketchbook across her knees, swept the pencil across one page, muttered, turned to a fresh one, muttered again.

"Can't get started?" Emily asked. She sat on the other end of the couch with her leather journal, trying to compose one note to her brother, another to Mona. "Is there such a thing as artist's block?"

"There is at the moment."

"Talk to me."

"I've been painting terror too long."

"Is the bucket empty?"

"I'm not taking it with me."

"Good. Fresh start."

"That's the thing. Starting a painting about someone else's story is easy. I just pick the scene that will make the most dramatic cover—freezing time at the perfect moment, catching the characters in mid-danger, mid-scream—"

"Mid-kiss?"

"Haven't painted many of those."

"Now's your chance." Emily stretched her arms above her head. "You know *our* story. Paint your favorite part, and we'll carry on from there." She thought for a second. "There's two, for me. One is kissing you at the fair. That alcove in the Court of the Moon. The light was magic."

"It was. I'd love to paint that." She tapped the pencil on her pad. "What's the other?"

"Dancing. You in that sleek blue satin number. Me in Neddy's suit—" She bit her lip. "Leave out the mustache? I wouldn't want to be stuck with *it* for decades."

"Definitely not."

"And let's dance somewhere else? Not Forbidden City. That scene didn't end well." She frowned. "Can you do that?"

"I can paint anything you can imagine."

"Then let me be your Scheherazade. I'll tell you our story—our story so far. You draw. I'll bet the painting takes form by the time you fall asleep."

"Alright." Haskel lit a cigarette. "How does it begin?"

"Once upon a time, there was a waif and a stray whose song enchanted a golden-haired painter." She cocked her head. "May I change a few details?"

"Be my guest."

"Good. They lived gloriously free, in a house with a bathroom and a real kitchen and a library with a big window—like Franny and Babs have—that looked out across the bay." She paused. "Your courtyard is nice, but if I'm picking my own fantasy, I'd rather have a view. Of moonlight. And the fair. Which does *not* close next week, please."

Haskel laughed as she filled a page with sketches. "I'll do my best."

"I feel like we're packing for a long trip."

"We are, in a way."

"Hmm. Then make sure you have cigarettes and bourbon, and we can get raspberry rings and coffee where we're going. Fried chicken seems to be universal, so no worries there. But maybe off in a corner, a big sack of money with a dollar sign, like the Monopoly man's? It might come in handy."

"That's a lot of detail for one painting."

"Well, you don't have to leave room for the magazine title or the story names. You can fit a lot more things in."

"Yes, ma'am." Haskel turned a page, scribbled a few notes. "Please do remember that if you become *too* bossy, I can still skip town, change my name to Millicent, and move to Des Moines without you."

"*Pffft.* Seems prudent to be quite specific when asking a magic rock for what my heart desires." She grinned. "Which is mostly you, but—oh! Lupo's."

Haskel nodded and turned another page, sketching and laughing as if their lives did not depend on this.

• • •

Four days later, the painting was almost complete. Haskel had barely slept. The other women had taken turns coming over with food and beer and cigarettes—and copies of the daily papers. No news, no progress by the police in locating the mystery man. One afternoon, Polly picked up Haskel's camera and used the last shot on that roll to capture them watching Haskel work.

"At least we'll have something to remember you by," Helen said, her light tone at odds with her melancholy expression. "I'll take the film to Owl Drug and get it developed."

It was Babs who knocked on the door Saturday morning. "I'm taking requests for supper," she said. She looked over at the drafting table. "Is it done?"

"Almost. I need to finish our faces, and then I've got a few bits of—" Haskel fumbled for a word.

"Mumbo-jumbo?" Babs said. "I've lived with Franny for ten years. I know the routine. Still don't have a firm grasp on what she *does*, exactly. Sounds like gibberish to me, but I can't deny it works. Drives the rational part of me half mad." She sat on the couch. "What do you need from us?"

"Is Polly done with the box?"

"She was fiddling when I went to bed last night, but I think so."

"Good. Ask everyone to come to dinner here tonight. We'll have a party before we—make our exit." She turned to Emily. "Chinese food?"

"No. This all started with Lupo's. Why break with tradition?"

"Brings it all full circle," Babs agreed. "I'll get two pies and bring some wine and a salad. What time?"

"Six. Make sure you have the box and any tools Polly will need to finish it up." She looked at the bookcase. "Oh, and ask Franny if she'd like that run of magazines for her library. Or anything else you want from here. We'll be traveling light."

They spent the afternoon boxing up the studio, saying goodbye to familiar books and clothes and furnishings they would not see again, if all went as planned. Then Haskel spread a cloth across the table for their feast. Helen arrived first, with a pink bakery box: tiny custard tarts and sweet Chinese buns filled with sesame and red bean paste. "Fong says sesame brings good luck," she said. "I figured we should cover all the bases."

Franny, Babs, and Polly appeared ten minutes later, laden with parcels—some fragrant with sausage and basil, the others redolent of varnish and glue. The table was soon covered with food, the wine opened, and the sounds of women talking and laughing—and occasionally singing—filled the room, echoing out into the courtyard until well after midnight.

When there was nothing left but crusts and dregs, Haskel stood. "It's time." She handed Franny the key to the studio. "Come back in the morning. If we're still here, it's all been a fool's errand."

"And if you're not," Polly said, "I'll put the last touches on a thaumaturgy that would impress even my father." She grinned. "Latin. Means 'work of wonder.'"

"Then we'll put it where it will be safe for—" Franny's voice shook, her eyes bright with both joy and sadness. "—for a long and wondrous adventure."

Leaving took another half hour. Hugs and tears and kissed cheeks, smiles and more tears.

When they were alone again, Haskel took Emily into her arms. "Are you ready for this?"

"I love you," she said. "I'd follow you to the end of the world. Any world."

They made love under the skylight. Just before dawn, they dressed in comfortable, favorite clothes. Haskel went to the drafting table and added the last details—eyes filled with joy, smiles on the two faces and, by habit, her bold signature in the corner. With an atomizer, she dusted the entire painting with the rest of the *tundér-pör*, giving it a kind of moonlit glow that shimmered for a moment before settling.

Carefully, she laid the art into the shallow box. It fit exactly, no room to slip or slide. She muttered words that Emily did not understand, then motioned to her. "A bit of you and a bit of me went *into* the pigment. To—close the circuit—we need some of the finished painting to bind us together." She wiped a finger across the tip of one corner of the paper and touched the iridescent powder to Emily's lips.

Emily did the same for her.

A few more arcane syllables. Haskel smiled and took her hands. "Now, kiss me, my love, and *bon voyage*."

. . .

Franny unlocked the door of the silent studio at noon. The painting lay in its wooden box, the lid open. A note next to it said simply:

> *Thanks.*
> —*Haskel*

"How do we know it's not a trick?" Polly looked around. "That they haven't just scarpered off to parts unknown?"

"We don't. But if it was misdirection, it was brilliantly done, don't you think?" Franny pointed to the bag of tools. "Hand me that spice tin. You and I have work to do."

TRICK OR TREAT

It was his.

Marty Blake hung the CLOSED sign in his window and pulled the blinds down so the shop was in darkness, save for a single halogen spot illuminating the wooden box.

He went to the back room, returning with a bottle of Courvoisier and a paper cup. The occasion called for a snifter, Waterford crystal at the very least, but this was all he had. There would be more celebrations later. He poured a generous slosh and raised a toast. "Haskel's last painting," he said aloud.

For the better part of an hour, he stood, sipping the cognac and gaping at his treasure. He still couldn't believe his luck. The artwork wasn't remotely what he'd imagined, late at night in the bar with the other dealers, talking about their fantasies, their dreams. But here it was. The Holy Grail.

Who would believe it?

No one, he thought. No bragging rights without proof. He had to document it, cover his ass for the insurance company. Then he'd post the photos. He smiled, imagining the fame and notoriety, the surge in business that was sure to follow. He opened a cupboard and retrieved his camera, a state-of-the-art digital SLR.

Marty stood directly over the box and took a few shots. None of them worked. He tried again, but no matter what the camera angle, the halogen spot glared off the thick glass. He turned it off and flicked on the fluorescents recessed in the ceiling, harsh, but diffuse. Five more shots. Shit. The sides of the box cast wide shadows. He stood on a chair, but there was always a dark line across part of the image.

Frustrated, he laid a book on the table. Maybe if the box were tilted, just an inch, he might be able to get a clear shot. As he began—oh so delicately—to raise one end, a few grains of blue pigment trickled to the bottom of the painting. He quickly laid it flat again.

It was a devilish problem. Could he lift the glass off? No. Its edges were sealed beneath the frame of the lid. Break the pane? No again. The shards would fall inward, onto the chalk surface. A glass cutter and suction cups? He'd seen that in a *Mission Impossible* movie, but lacked both the tools and the know-how. And if the whole *sheet* of glass fell in—? Marty shuddered.

He poured more liquor and stared helplessly. Someone had sealed the box; there *must* be a way to open it. He focused his brightest LED magnifier on every surface. Nothing. He sat down wearily; as the light wavered in his hand, it caught an odd reflection. He squinted. Two hidden hinges, *inside,* cleverly painted to match the walls of the box. Aha!

Using an X-Acto knife, he scraped at the outer surface directly behind the hardware. A flake of what looked like old cellophane fluttered to the tabletop, revealing a hairline seam. *Eureka!* He inserted the tip of the razor-sharp knife and followed the line around two corners, wiping bits of gelatinous gum off the blade until he hit an obstacle.

Front and center, under the thin lip of the lid, invisible in its shadow, was a tiny metal bar. Its color was only a fraction of a shade darker than the surrounding wood, set so perfectly flush with the surface that his gloved fingertips had failed to register the difference.

Ingenious.

He braced one hand behind the box and leaned down to peer closely at the secret latch. His hand trembled as he pressed his right thumb onto the spot.

A muffled click sounded as the mechanism engaged. The lid sprang open with startling violence. He jerked back, screaming as his face was enveloped by a hideous, eddying blackness that stung like a thousand tiny wasps.

With a terrible, savage force, Martin Blake began to sneeze.

Acknowledgments

I fell in love with San Francisco in 1963 (I was eight). I moved there in 1976, and a year later wrote the first lines of a story that would become *Passing Strange*. They did not survive, but forty years later, the story of Emily Netterfield and Loretta Haskel is finally on the page. As I type this, my desk is littered with dozens of books about the city, View-Master reels of the fair, WPA guides and maps, and souvenirs from before I was born. I am especially grateful to the GLBT Archives for oral histories and photos of Mona's; to Trina Robbins and Arthur Dong for their amazing books on the history of Forbidden City and other Chinese nightclubs; to Stephen D. Korshak and J. David Spurlock for their work on the art of Margaret Brundage; to Mara's Italian Pastry for raspberry rings (it was research . . .); and to Grant Canfield, my poker buddy, for letting me spend hours looking through his vast collection of vintage pulps. Last, but certainly not least, thanks to Lee Harris and Irene Gallo, for founding Tor.com's novella line, and to Jonathan Strahan, editor extraordinaire, who suggested I might want to write one for him.

About the Author

Photograph by Scott R. Kline

ELLEN KLAGES is the author of two acclaimed historical novels: *The Green Glass Sea,* which won the Scott O'Dell Award, and the New Mexico Book Award; and *White Sands, Red Menace,* which won the California and New Mexico Book Awards. Her story, "Basement Magic," won a Nebula Award and *Wakulla Springs,* coauthored with Andy Duncan, was nominated for the Nebula, Hugo, and Locus Awards, and won the World Fantasy Award for Best Novella. She lives in San Francisco, in a small house full of strange and wondrous things.

TOR·COM

Science fiction. Fantasy. The universe.

And related subjects.

*

More than just a publisher's website, *Tor.com* is a venue for **original fiction, comics,** and **discussion** of the entire field of SF and fantasy, in all media and from all sources. Visit our site today—and join the conversation yourself.